THE BIGGEST CHRISTMAS SECRET EVER

Also by L.D. Lapinski

Stepfather Christmas

Jamie

Artezans: The Forgotten Magic

The Strangeworlds Travel Agency

Book 1: The Strangeworlds Travel Agency

Book 2: Edge of the Ocean

Book 3: The Secrets of the Stormforest

A Very Strangeworlds Christmas (ebook only)

Adventure in the Floating Mountains (World Book Day Title)

THE BIGGEST CHRISTMAS SECRET EVER

L. D. LAPINSKI

Orion

ORION CHILDREN'S BOOKS

First published in Great Britain in 2024 by
Hodder & Stoughton

10 9 8 7 6 5 4 3 2 1

A CIP catalogue record for this book is
available from the British Library.

ISBN 978 1 510 11305 3

Typeset in Baskerville by Palimpsest Book
Production Limited, Falkirk, Stirlingshire

Printed and bound in Great Britain by Clays
Ltd, Elcograf S.p.A.

The paper and board used in this book are
made from wood from responsible sources.

Orion Children's Books
An imprint of Hachette Children's Group
Part of Hodder & Stoughton Limited
Carmelite House
50 Victoria Embankment
London EC4Y 0DZ

An Hachette UK Company
www.hachette.co.uk
wwww.hachettechildrens.co.uk

For Roscoe
a new story for
a new baby

One

There aren't many people who can burp to the tune of *Jingle Bells*, but my brother somehow managed it. He even took a bow when he got to the end.

Me and Mum stared at him, our expressions somewhere between horrified and impressed. 'So . . . that's what you learnt instead of your GCSE French verbs,' Mum said after a moment.

'Time well spent, I think,' said Will, patting his chest as he folded his lanky teenage self into a chair. 'I'm going to show Nick when he gets home.'

'I'm sure he'll be very entertained,' Mum said, sipping her coffee. She looked back at her pile of case notes. She'd only been back at work full time for a couple of months, and already it was as though she'd never left. Endless emails about cats who'd got into fights with bigger cats, hamsters who wouldn't eat and fish that seemed to do nothing but poop pinged on to her tablet constantly – and the pages of notes she brought home in her rucksack never seemed to get any smaller. Mum always said how much she loved her job, but it was hard work being a vet. I'd already made up my mind not to be one.

But even with her busy workload, Mum had found time to dive completely into her usual enthusiasm for decorating the house for Christmas. Every year she dug out handmade baubles, toilet-roll angels and scrunched-up paper snowflakes from years gone by. Our boring living room was transformed in the space of a few hours into a grotto of fairy lights, glow-in-the-dark reindeer and a seven-foot-tall Christmas tree that dominated one corner of the already cramped space. The picture frames on the windowsill were buried beneath glittery fluff that smelled of dust but was sparklingly festive. Christmas in our house was always the *best* time of year.

'Harper, are you sitting on my wool?' Will asked. 'I've told you not to mess with my stuff.'.

'I wouldn't dream of messing with your stuff,' I said, rolling my eyes. 'Don't get your needles in a twist. I stuck it in this carrier bag, because it was in the way. Again.'

'Like your laundry,' Mum added, muttering something about lost socks under her breath.

Will ignored us both, and grabbed the bag to put it out of my reach. He wasn't as grumpy as he pretended to be. He'd taught himself to knit a few months ago after watching a video on YouTube, and now could make lumpy shapeless bags that he claimed were hats, or mittens or socks. His big project was a Christmas jumper that he'd started knitting in summer but still hadn't finished. With December now underway, it looked as though it would have to be a Christmas hanky.

Outside, a car's headlights approached, and Mum glanced up expectantly and then back at her work when the lights passed by. We were all *waiting*, trying to find something to do without leaving the living room. The TV was on silent, the subtitles scrolling along the bottom of the screen as a chef made caramelised vegetables, so sugar-coated they rolled about in the oven tray like lumps of seaside rock.

'He's late,' I said.

'He'll be here,' Mum said. 'He always is, in the end.'

It was true, he always was.

As if on cue, there was another flash of headlights in the front window, and then a vehicle pulled on to the drive. Will darted over and yanked across the net curtain enough for me to see a red pick-up truck. 'He's here!'

'I told you so,' Mum smiled, taking her reading glasses off and fluffing out her blonde hair.

There was the sound of keys in the back door, a heavy thud of boots on the kitchen mat, a clunk of a suitcase and then a booming cry of: 'I'm ho-ho-hoooome!'

I darted around the sofa and through the door, grinning my head off.

Nick stood in the kitchen, hands on his hips, a scarf around his neck and shoulders, a big smile on his bearded face. He was wearing dark blue jeans and heavy black boots as he always did, his white and grey beard was trim and neat compared to the flyaway hair on his head that had been haphazardly pulled back into a bun, and the buttons on his red coat were straining to remain fastened over his barrelled torso. 'Harper!' he said delightedly, as soon as he saw me.

'Nick!' I went over for a hug, and he lifted me clean off the ground.

'I think you've grown again these past two weeks,' he said after a moment, planting me back on the floor. 'You're always doing that.'

'Not as much as Will,' I said, looking at my fifteen-year-old brother who was creeping into the kitchen, pretending not to be bothered about Nick's arrival but failing to hide a smile.

'Hey, Nick,' he managed to drawl.

'Hey, Will.' The two of them bumped fists, and I hid a smirk behind my hand. It would take Will another hour or two to forget about trying to be an adult.

Finally, Mum came in, smiling and with her arms stretched out. She and Nick had a big cuddle and a disgusting kiss. 'You're late,' she chided as they broke apart.

'You should have seen the traffic,' Nick said. 'It was fine until we got over the North Sea . . . and then you wouldn't believe the flocks of migrating birds! The girls

6

had to dodge left and right. Mind you, they were glad to stretch their legs.'

'Did you get them all tucked away?' Mum asked.

'Oh yes. Eight reindeer all safe and sound at the farm park,' Nick chuckled. 'They were settling down for sleep when I left. The quick flight from Finland was enough to give them a reminder of what's to come in a few weeks.'

'I still can't believe we can just talk about all this now,' I said happily. 'After you two keeping it a secret for so long.'

'Well, can you blame us?' Mum scoffed, as Nick laughed. 'Imagine if I had told you I was dating Father Christmas the first time you'd met Nick – you never would have believed me! You would have thought I was trying to be funny.'

'But he *is* Father Christmas!' I cried happily.

And it was true. He had the beard, the strength, the

reindeer, the sleigh *and the magic*. Nick didn't just look like Santa Claus – he *was* Santa Claus. The real one. The one and only. And it was the biggest secret ever . . .

It had all started the Christmas before last. I'd had my suspicions about Nick straight away, because there were plenty of clues – the snowfall that only seemed to land in our garden, and the morning we found a reindeer on the roof! But it was only through some cunning detective work, a few broken promises, and a night I'll never forget that the truth finally came out. We didn't just have a sort-of-stepdad. We had Stepfather Christmas!

Things had gotten interesting after that. Last Christmas, the first one with the secret out in the family, it had been funny rather than mysterious: how there were endless boxes of post for Nick, and how he knew what was inside every wrapped present. I'd hoped for a magical Christmas Eve flight in the sleigh again, helping to deliver a few presents . . . but that night there had been torrential rain so it was too wet for me and Will to join Nick and his reindeer.

But then, in the new year, we all got a surprise . . .

There was a sudden wail from a chunky white walkie-talkie on the kitchen counter. The wail quietened off, and then turned into a sort of nonsense babble.

'Oh, she's awake,' Mum said.

'I'll go,' Nick said, easing past her and heading up the stairs.

Me and Will exchanged looks. A lot had changed this past year. Some of it had been small, some of it had been big – and one bit was absolutely spectacular.

'Here she is!' Nick said, coming back into the kitchen. There was a baby on his hip, clinging to his coat with her fierce little hands, looking around at us sleepily. Nick kissed her on the head. 'I missed you, Yula Hall.'

Two

Oh yeah, we have a baby sister!

I don't mean to brag, but Yula is, without a doubt, the cutest and best baby sister there has ever been in the entire universe. She's round and squishy and has blonde wispy hair that sticks up in all directions like she's a cartoon scientist. Yula's voice has a good range – she makes little sing-song noises and can also bellow louder than a foghorn. She can crawl and pull herself upright on the furniture, and everything she set eyes on goes into her mouth. She's not quite eleven months old, but nevertheless she completely rules our house.

Nick covered Yula in kisses, until she decided she'd had enough of his whiskers brushing against her cheek and grabbed a fistful of his beard. He went very still as she clung on with a vice-like grip. 'Ouch.'

Yula beamed and yanked harder. Nick's eyes started to water.

'She does that with my hair, too,' I said, wincing in sympathy.

Yula finally decided to let go, and gave a happy squeal, kicking her legs enthusiastically. She wasn't ready for walking quite yet, but she was doing plenty of leg exercises in preparation. Mum was busy baby-proofing the house from top to bottom. Will already had a lock on his door.

'Come and sit down, Nick, you've had a long flight,' Mum said, leading the way into the glittering living room.

I decided to put the kettle on to give Nick and Mum

a moment with Yula by themselves. The problem with Nick's job was that sometimes he had to go back to the North Pole for a few weeks at a time. The official story for anyone who asked was that Nick spent time in Finland for work. Which was actually true, we just didn't mention the Father Christmas part. And we had learnt that there were all sorts of Christmassy things Nick had to be a part of before December: like toy manufacturing and delivery, sleigh improvements, caring for reindeer calves, dealing with emergencies at T.I.N.S.E.L. (The International NorthPole Sorting Envelopes Logistics division, which handled the redirection of all the letters) . . . being Father Christmas was a job all year, not just on Christmas Eve. But even though it was tricky to organise sometimes, Nick made sure to come back to the UK at least once every two weeks to be with us. He'd promised he would and, so far, he was making good on it.

Mum had taken time off when Yula was first born,

13

but now that she was back to work full time, she was as busy as ever. Plus, Yula had be picked up from nursery before Mum's old finishing time, so now all of Mum's forms and veterinary notes came home with her to complete in the evenings. And she had to fit those around looking after Yula. Our lives had changed a lot, but it was a good kind of busy – the sort where there's always something to look forward to.

Will brought his knitting bag in from the lounge and started sorting out his needles. The half-a-jumper he was working on dangled between them. 'Maybe this jumper can be for Yula,' he said, holding it up and looking at the size of it.

'Or a hamster,' I suggested, pouring water into the teapot. I piled digestive biscuits on to a plate and put it on the tea tray. 'Why don't you stick to making hats? The hats are great.' The hats were *not* great, but they were very warm, despite looking like misshapen puddings. We all had one now, even Yula – though hers was miles too big for her.

'I just wanted to try to do something a bit more complicated . . .' Will started counting stitches. 'Knitting is meant to be good for your brain, so I thought it would help me with my Puzzle Cubing. I didn't realise it was going to consume my entire life.' He accepted his tea with a smile and frowned down at his project. I left him to it. The patterns looked more complicated than the coding lessons we had at school.

In the living room, Nick and Mum were watching Yula speed-crawl from one end of the room to the other. Everything looked very cosy. The Christmas tree was illuminated and twinkling with colourful fairy lights that seemed more sparkly than ever, making the framed pictures on the windowsill glow brightly. There were photos of me, Will, Mum and Nick at Lapland; Yula, five minutes after she'd been born when she still looked like an angry turnip; Mum and Nick at the seaside; me and Will dressed up in a lot of padded gear to play Laser Tag; and me on my twelfth birthday going to see the Rainbow Catz at the East Midlands Arena.

'How were things at the North Pole, Nick?' I asked, putting the tea tray down.

Nick gave a resigned sort of groan. 'Busy. The sleigh is still over there − the tech team at HQ want to make some anti-drone modifications. People keep inventing new technology that I have to try and avoid . . .'

I wanted to laugh − it was funny to think of Father Christmas trying to avoid being spotted by a drone, swerving around the skies. With all the satellites and cameras around, it was a wonder he managed to get away without being detected at all. 'Don't you *ever* get seen?' I asked.

'Occasionally. It's not *always* a problem. It depends who I'm seen by,' he said, reaching for one of the biscuits that had silently transformed into Christmas-tree shapes the moment I brought them into the room. 'Children see me flying past? No problem. Someone films me on their phone? Huge incident.'

'What happens then?' I asked, imagining alarms and flashing lights and elves in jumpsuits running towards helicopters.

'The communications team usually make sure it's dismissed as a hoax,' Nick said, dipping his biscuit. 'They have elves posing as human video experts who claim the footage has been altered. It's a bit of a fib, but necessary . . . if everyone figured out who and where I am, Christmas could be ruined.'

'*I* figured it out,' I said, a bit smugly.

'Yes, but you're smart,' Nick said. 'And I *was* living in your house, which gave you a little advantage.'

'But what if someone else figures it out?' I asked. 'Like, a stranger?'

Nick lifted Yula on to his lap, and she promptly stole the last half of his biscuit. 'I don't even like to think about it,' he said. 'That could mean the end of Christmas as we know it.'

Three

I was woken by the familiar delicious scent of gingerbread drifting through the air from the kitchen. I smiled into my pillow, feeling like Christmas had truly begun. Nick's festive biscuits were always perfect – the right balance of crunchy and soft, the spices just ideal, the amount of chocolate chips just what you wanted. And he never used a shape cutter, either – just traced a flat knife through the dough into the exact shape he wanted, and they never went all blobby in the oven like when me and Will tried to do snowmen and they came out looking like shortbread splats.

I let my nose lead me downstairs. Mum had gone to work already and Will never rose before ten at weekends, so it was just Nick and Yula downstairs, the older trying to get the younger to eat a bit of Wheaty Bricks cereal.

'Nnnnnn!' Yula braced herself on the tray of her highchair and leaned away from the spoon as if it held horrors beyond human comprehension.

'I don't blame her,' I said. 'The house smells of biscuits and you want her to try something that looks like it's already been eaten once.'

Nick sighed and held the spoon out persistently. 'Are all babies like this?' he asked.

'No idea,' I said, fishing out a box of cereal. 'Don't you see a lot of babies on Christmas Eve?'

'They're usually asleep.' Nick decided to eat the spoonful of soggy wheat himself and gave a big false smile. 'Delicious! . . . If you don't have a sense of taste,' he added.

Yula made grabbing gestures at the plate of buttered toast on the table, and Nick put some on the tray of her highchair. She promptly picked up two pieces and wiped them into her hair. Nick put his head in his hands.

'Good luck,' I said brightly, balancing a Christmas biscuit on top of my cereal and taking the whole thing into the living room. If Yula saw I was eating Coco-Frosted Crispies she'd shatter the windows screaming until she got some.

*

Since Mum was at work, we were going to spend most of the day with Nick at his job – or, at least, the job he used as a cover story whilst he was incognito. We took the long route through the village so we could call into the library and the post office, get Yula settled at the new childminder, and, most importantly, call into the cake shop.

The council had put the village Christmas lights up at the end of November, and they glowed dimly in the

December morning. There was going to be a parade on Christmas Eve to raise money for charity, and there were posters all over the village advertising stalls, games, a raffle and a very special visitor.

'Nick, look!' Will grinned as he pointed out the posters. There was a photograph of a man dressed as Father Christmas sitting on the back of a lorry that had been decorated to look like a sleigh, if you stood about thirty metres away. The man was waving at the camera, his big fake beard over his nose and almost in his eyes.

Nick snorted. 'Whose beard grows from their bottom eyelids?' he muttered, giving the well-meaning imposter a good look. Yula, strapped to his chest in the baby carrier, kicked her legs and made sing-song noises as Christmas music started blasting out of the doorway of the nearest shop doorway. Nick smiled. 'It's not a bad attempt overall though, actually. He just needs to sort that beard out.'

'Does it feel weird?' I asked quietly. 'Seeing people dressed like you?'

'It's somewhere between weird and flattering,' Nick said. 'It's always happened, though. And the important thing is, they mean well – they're bringing happiness to children all over the world. And a great many of them accept letters that then get passed on to the T.I.N.S.E.L. network. They're an essential part of the chain that links back to the North Pole – and to me.'

'I'm surprised they didn't ask *you* to star on the posters!' A jovial adult's voice made us all turn. Mr Tipling, of Tipling's World of Tipples – the wine shop on the high street – was giving Nick a wink and a smile as he indicated the poster. 'You'd be perfect for the job, if I do say so!'

Nick gave a single bark of a laugh. 'Ha. You're too kind.'

Yula blew a raspberry.

'Sorry, you must get that all the time,' Mr Tipling

chuckled. 'Still, make sure you go and get a raffle ticket or five from Milly Feuille at the cake shop. And don't miss the big parade on Christmas Eve – we're raising money for the local children's hospital charity, so we want to raise as much money as we possibly can!' Mr Tipling gave a cheery wave and carried on down the street saying good morning to everyone he saw.

Will shook his head. 'He's too happy for this time in the morning.'

'Some of us have been awake more than an hour, William,' I pointed out.

'He's got a kind heart,' Nick said. 'You can't fault his charitable attitude.'

We made it to the childminder, and handed Yula over to a smiling woman who promised to let us know if Yula didn't settle, before carrying on down the road, heading to the farm park via the bakery. Will got a jam doughnut, Nick a slice of chocolate cake and I had a custard slice.

We were just debating whether to eat them on the way or after we got to the farm, when Nick's phone rang.

'Bother.' Nick handed his paper bag to Will as he struggled to extract his phone. He looked at the number on the screen and frowned. 'It's Yula's childminder,' he said. 'She's only been there ten minutes, maybe she keeps crying, poor thing.' He swiped the screen and put the phone to his ear. 'Hello?'

There was a pause as the staff spoke to Nick. Me and Will shrugged at one another. Maybe Yula was missing us, or perhaps she'd got wet or sandy, or had decided to wear her snack rather than eat it. If there was one thing we'd learnt recently, it was that babies didn't stay neat and tidy for long.

'Alright, thank you, we'll be right there.' Nick hung up, his face a strange mask of incredulity. 'We need to go pick her up,' he said.

'What's wrong?' Will asked.

'I'm not sure yet,' Nick said. 'Apparently the babies were playing outside, and when the staff turned around she was just covered in it.'

'Covered in what?' I asked. Mud? Sand? Something worse?

Nick looked at me. 'Covered in . . . snow.'

Four

Snow?

Snow?

I glanced at Will as we hurried back up the road to the childminder's, under a clear blue sky. I had a feeling that *this* December was going to end up being rather eventful, too. By the look on Will's face, he thought the same. I couldn't resist a little secret wriggle of glee at the idea.

At the childminder's, the owner, Miss Bittern, was standing anxiously at the doors, holding a plastic bag.

Around her, the windows of the building were decorated with Christmas lights, cotton-wool snow and baby handprints arranged like snowflakes stuck on to the glass.

'We got Yula warm and dry straight away,' she said as soon as she saw us. She looked horrified at the idea of a child in her care being even remotely damp for a second. 'She's in her spare clothes, these ones are freezing cold and wet – as is her coat.' She handed the carrier bag to Nick, whose face was carefully blank.

'You said that Yula was . . . in the snow?' he asked calmly.

Miss Bittern nodded frantically, her head bobbing in a blur. 'Outside, in the sandpit!' She pressed a hand to her chest as if unable to imagine anything worse. 'One moment she was happily digging in the sand, the next moment there she was buried in snow from head to toe! We have no idea how it happened, we're so sorry!'

'Don't apologise,' Nick said, still friendly. 'I'm sure it

was just one of those freak weather events. Climate change, you know?'

'Oh, I *do* know,' Miss Bittern said, clinging to the offered excuse like a life-raft. 'It must have been a strange cloud passing over . . . Yula was laughing and patting the snow, so I don't think she was upset, but we thought you should know all the same, in case you wanted to take her home.'

'Oh yes, I think we will on this occasion,' said Nick. 'Make sure she's not . . . We'll just make sure she's alright. Thank you so much for calling.'

'Of course. I'll just fetch her for you . . .' Miss Bittern hurried away.

Nick, Will and I exchanged silent, knowing looks. Snow that appeared from nowhere had happened to us before. We'd stepped out of the back door to find our garden – and *only* our garden – knee-deep in snow. Nowhere else on the street had been touched, not so much as a snowflake. Later on we found out that the snow had actually been caused by Nick's low-flying reindeer on a practice run before Christmas Eve!

'Has anything been flying overhead that should be at the farm park?' I muttered to Nick.

Nick's eyes swept over the sky. 'No chance. Besides, it's daytime. They can only fly by night.'

So, if the snow hadn't been caused by flying reindeer then . . .

'Here she is!' Miss Bittern was back, carrying Yula. She was bundled up in her coat and spare clothes and looked as happy as a pig in muck (or a baby in snow). She beamed when she saw Nick and reached for him to take her. 'She can come back for her next session if she doesn't get the sniffles,' Miss Bittern said, giving Yula's rucksack full of snacks and nappies to Will.

'Thank you, we'll keep an eye on her,' Nick said. Yula kicked her legs and made singing noises as she snuggled into Nick's red coat. 'See you tomorrow, Miss Bittern.'

We all said goodbye and walked with Yula back on to the high street, heading down to Farmer Llama's Petting Zoo and Garden Centre. It was a cold day, for sure, but the sky was still a clear biting blue with no sign of any dark snow clouds at all. Nick kept glancing at Yula, but she was oblivious to the mood, waving at every dog she saw and chewing on her own fist in turns.

She was certainly none the worse for being found covered in snow. But where *had* that snow come from?

At Farmer Llama's, Nick apologised for being late to work, but no one seemed to mind as he'd brought his cute baby with him. Yula sat on the shop counter like she was waiting to be scanned and gift-wrapped, picking up every little pencil and wind-up toy on the desk as Nick explained what had happened and asked the shop manager if he could keep her with him for the day.

'That's no problem,' Angie said. 'We should have babies visit all the time, they're a joy.'

31

'Until it's nappy-change time,' Will muttered. Yula's face had gone very serious as she concentrated hard on something.

Nick picked her up quickly. 'We'll meet you at the paddock,' he said to me and Will, holding Yula at arm's length and marching straight towards the toilets.

Will and I headed over to the reindeer. I loved going with Nick to his 'day job' – visiting a farm park and petting some reindeer was always a treat.

Thunder and Lightning trotted over as soon as we arrived, sniffing our pockets for raisins and biscuits. I scratched them both on their woolly noses. Nick's reindeer were big – bigger than you might have expected – more like stocky horses with antlers, and they were covered in wiry grey-brown fur. They wore red harnesses with jingle bells on whilst they were staying at the farm park, but when was time for them to get to their real work, Nick would kit them out with tough leather reins strong enough to pull a fully-loaded sleigh.

Will pulled out the playpen (or baby prison) that Nick kept at the farm park for emergencies, and when Nick returned with a smiling Yula he plopped her into it. She immediately pulled herself standing and yelled for freedom.

I left the reindeer at the fence and went over. 'So . . . what caused the snow?' I asked Nick, now that it was just the four of us. 'If it wasn't the reindeer, was it really freak weather?'

'Get real,' Will snorted. 'It's not cold enough to snow, not by a long shot.'

'So, what was it then?'

Nick was staring at Yula, a tiny hint of a smile beginning to play at the corners of his mouth. 'I think . . .' he said slowly, 'I think it might have been her.'

Five

A few hours later, we were all watching Yula, who was sitting on the dining table-top like a sort of specimen. She was chewing her rubber giraffe toy and making burbling noises. Nothing unusual there. We'd come home as soon as we could, using Yula as an excuse to leave the farm park early. After his declaration about the baby, Nick had fed and watered the reindeer in silence, and then we walked home without saying much either, just holding Yula's hands as she babbled, strapped to Nick's front.

'I still don't get what you mean,' Will said. 'She's a baby, not a storm cloud.'

Nick was stroking his beard thoughtfully. 'Where else could the snow have come from,' he said, 'unless she made it herself? I wonder . . .'

Yula bashed the rubber giraffe on the table and howled like a tiny chubby Godzilla.

'I wonder . . . if she has Christmas magic.'

Will and me looked up at Nick, our mouths dropping open like simultaneous drawbridges. 'Whaaaa?' we managed.

Nick took a deep breath. 'Christmas magic is hereditary,' he said slowly. 'It gets passed down in my family. But it doesn't necessarily follow a straight line – just because your parent was Santa Claus doesn't mean you will inherit their magic; it could go from a grandparent to a grandchild, from an uncle to a niece—'

'Niece?' Will interrupted. 'Isn't Santa Claus always a man?'

36

'Of course not,' Nick snorted. 'Father Christmas, Santa Claus, Kris Kringle . . . there've been lots of names and dozens of different looks. Santa Claus is the embodiment of the magic of Christmas. They don't have to be a certain kind of person or look a specific kind of way. It's me, for the time being, but one day it will be someone else's turn.'

'Someone else's turn . . .' I repeated, my gaze sliding to Yula, who was trying to pull one of the giraffe's legs off. 'But you can't surely mean what I think you're saying?!'

Nick nodded. 'The time comes – for everyone who does the job – when it's your turn to eventually retire. There's no set period of service, but a successor is always ready and waiting when the time is right.' He stared at Yula affectionately. 'I think my successor has turned up.'

Will's mouth was flapping silently as he tried to regain the ability to make sounds and words. My mind felt like it was going through a Christmas-themed washing machine. It had been difficult enough to make peace with the fact that Nick, our mum's boyfriend, was Father Christmas. To find out that my baby sister had Christmas magic *and* might actually *be* Santa one day, was a whole other firework in my brain.

Yula chuckled as she lobbed her giraffe across the kitchen, then burped loudly. It smelled like candy canes.

'But . . . But what's going to happen?' I asked.

'It's nothing to worry about!' Nick said quickly. 'I promise you. She'll learn to control it, and she'll be just like everyone else as she grows up. Then, when it's time for her to take over the job, she'll know. We both will.'

'My baby sister has Christmas magic and is the future Santa.' Will finally found his voice. He stared at her for a few seconds, his face twisting into wide-eyed disbelief. 'I think I need a hot chocolate.'

'I think we all do,' Nick said kindly. He picked Yula

up and carried her with him over to the cupboards, hunting out his special tin of Finnish dark chocolate flakes.

'But she can't be Santa!' I said, staring at the table where Yula had been. 'She's a baby! A baby girl!'

'You don't always get to choose who you are,' Nick said vaguely, putting a pan on the stove. 'But that's for years in the future anyway. Right now, we just need to love her and look after her and keep her safe.'

Will shook himself then started to help, getting the oat milk out of the fridge. I watched them with a weird detachment. Yula was trying to grab the tin of chocolate like any baby would. Maybe Nick was mistaken.

When the hot chocolate was ready, and Nick had garnished each mug with a heap of squirty cream and a tiny gingerbread tree, Mum came through the door. She was carrying a huge bag of files and was still wearing her vet's scrubs.

'Oh, lovely,' she beamed as the chocolate smell hit her in the face. 'You must have read my mind, this is exactly what I need—'

'Yula made it snow today,' Will said bluntly, picking up his mug.

'What's that?' Mum asked, going over to coo at the baby. 'Did you do a snowy craft at your new childminders, my little Yula-poola?'

'Mum, I mean it *literally*,' Will insisted. 'She made snow appear from thin air!'

'Don't be silly, Will, I'm too tired for stories,' Mum said, taking the baby from Nick who was looking slightly stressed out. Mum registered his expression. 'What? What is it?'

Nick forced a smile. 'Um. Will is being serious, Helen.'

Mum blinked rapidly. 'What do you mean?'

Yula answered the question by sneezing loudly. Glittery snowflakes flew out of her nose, sparkling in the light for a second before melting in thin air and falling to the kitchen floor as tiny droplets.

Mum's mouth dropped open like a fish trying to sing opera.

Yula gave a happy squeal and waved her chubby fists.

'See?' Will said weakly.

Mum turned Yula around to hold her up and look her in the face. 'What did you just *do*?' she asked her.

Yula blew a raspberry and then laughed.

Mum kept her at eye level as she sank into the closest dining chair, her legs giving way in slow motion. 'Is this real?' Yula bounced her feet on Mum's legs like she was a trampoline, then reached for the tiny gingerbread tree in Nick's hot chocolate.

Nick handed it to her. 'It's real. As real as Christmas.'

'But . . .' Mum's eyes flicked from Yula to Nick and back again. 'Is − is this because of you?'

'Well, yes,' Nick said, blushing a little. 'She gets it from me.'

Mum tucked Yula's head under her chin as if she might melt just like the snowflakes, and snuggled her closely. 'Is she going to be OK?'

'She's going to be *fine*,' Nick said firmly, and no one could doubt his sincerity. 'She will be entirely fine. More than fine, even. She'll grow into it.'

Mum nodded, giving Yula another cuddle. 'Well, aren't you special, little bean?' Yula ignored her, focused on chewing the gingerbread with grim determination.

'And most importantly, she's got us, so everything will be alright,' Nick said. He handed me my mug and gave me a squeeze on the shoulder. 'It's just one of the things that makes her special. Makes our whole *family* special.'

I let go of a breath I hadn't realised I was holding. Nick was right. Our family was pretty complicated already but we managed fine. And Yula's bigger future sparkled somewhere far in the distance. We could handle Yula having a little Christmas magic for now, couldn't we?

Yula took the opportunity to grab a handful of squirty cream from the top of Mum's drink, and everyone laughed. Some things would never change.

Just then, there was a knock at the door.

Six

I went to answer the door, glad to have a little minute by myself. OK, so my sister *was* magical. But that wasn't scary, that was amazing! Maybe she'd make it snow especially for us on Christmas Day, so we could all build a snowman together. Maybe she could turn broccoli into candy canes, that would be a bonus.

The knock at the door came again, brisker this time, as though the person on the other side was impatient to be seen. I frowned. This wasn't our usual postie – she never rapped on the woodwork like that.

I went to unlock the door . . . then thought twice and put the chain on, before opening the door a crack. 'Hello?'

'Good afternoon, human child Harper Hall,' a snooty voice that seemed to come straight through someone's nose sounded through the gap. I could just about make out a smart suit, a clipboard and extremely shiny polished shoes that were so pointy they looked like weapons.

Human child?

'Who is it?' I asked.

The speaker ignored my question and instead replied, 'I'm looking for . . .' There was a pause, and a nasal sort of squeak as if they were unsure whether I could be trusted or not. 'I am looking for . . . Nicholas . . .'

The uncertainty in the voice made my stomach go all squirmy. No one around here called him *Nicholas.* I suddenly felt sure that whoever it was at our door knew the truth about Nick. But the only people supposed to know were us. I hesitated. 'Just . . . give me a second,' I said, shutting the door again before they could argue.

I went back into the kitchen, where everyone was fussing over Yula as she babbled merrily. I tugged on Nick's sleeve.

'Everything alright, Harps?' he asked. Seeing my face, he frowned. 'You've gone ever so pale. Who was it at the door?'

'They're still there,' I said. 'They asked for you. They asked for . . . Nicholas.' I shrugged.

Nick's smile fell slightly. 'Ah. I think I know who's here . . .' He looked at Mum. 'Helen, I think someone from . . . my real job . . . is here.'

Mum blinked but recovered quickly. 'Oh, I see. Well, invite them in.' She looked resignedly at the bags of paperwork on the table, the clothes drying on the radiators and the hot chocolate saucepan in the sink. I don't understand why grown-ups mind about mess when someone comes round – it just proves someone lives in the house, if you ask me.

I followed Nick to the door, standing in the hallway so I could see what was happening. Nick took the chain off the door and opened it.

Outside stood a woman in a smart purple suit jacket and skirt, those vicious-looking high-heeled patent shoes on her feet. Her hair was also purple, the colour of Parma Violets, and was styled into a lumpy beehive that rose up from her head in a cone. She had a pair of golden winged glasses perched on her nose, and a tiny pinched mouth that looked like a cat's bottom. There was an embroidered patch on the pocket of her jacket: a gold emblem with the letters E.S.D. in the middle of it.

She gave a salute. 'Sergeant Mistle, sir! Elf and Safety Department, sir! Here to investigate an incident of Unauthorised Magical Demonstration, sir!'

It was amazing how she could speak in capital letters.

Her saluting knocked her pile of hair to one side, and I caught a glimpse of her ears – pointy, just like her shoes. She wasn't a human at all, she was an elf.

Nick beckoned Sergeant Mistle inside, looking about to see if any of the neighbours had noticed the weird saluting woman, but thankfully there was no one else about. He swiftly shut the door behind her. Sergeant Mistle had her pen and clipboard at the ready and was gazing around the hallway as if she'd stepped into a condemned building. She looked at me. 'Is this your primary place of residence, human child?'

I didn't know what to say, so looked at Nick.

He gave me an *it's alright, I'll handle this* face, and then smiled at Sergeant Mistle. 'Why don't you come through into the living room?'

Sergeant Mistle's expression said that she'd rather not, but she gave a tight little nod anyway, and stepped delicately over some of Yula's discarded toy animals, following Nick into the kitchen. Just through the doorway, she froze, her blue eyes goggling.

'Hello there, I'm Helen,' Mum said brightly, coming forward with a hand held out ready to shake. Yula was in her highchair, carefully ripping up some important-looking papers, Will was elbow-deep in the washing up and there were still socks and pants all over the radiators.

Sergeant Mistle held out her pen, and Mum ended up shaking hands with that instead. 'Do *all of you* live here?' the sergeant asked. 'In this . . . drab little house?'

'Excuse me?' Mum asked, her smile vanishing instantly and her voice dropping an octave.

'This way!' Nick said loudly, steering Sergeant Mistle by her clipboard into the lounge before anything else could be said. He sat her down in the armchair beside the Christmas tree, and everyone else followed in, piling on to the sofa to stare at her. Will still had his rubber gloves on.

Sergeant Mistle gave the Christmas tree and the

decorations strung around the room an approving glance – the first time she'd looked pleased to see something since she came inside. She drew what looked like a tick on her clipboard.

'Who *are* you, exactly?' Mum asked, clearly still offended over the comment about the house. Yula was on her knee, diligently continuing to rip up the paperwork.

'My name is Sergeant Tosie Mistle,' the woman squeaked, primly. 'I am part of the North Pole's Elf and Safety Department, established in the year 350. I am here to investigate an alert we received about unauthorised use of Christmas magic.' Her eyes drifted to Yula, who was burbling away as she scattered the shreds of paper like falling snow. 'Whose baby is that?'

Mum and Nick looked at each other.

Sergeant Mistle gave a nod. 'I see. What is her name?'

'Yula,' Mum said, her arms around my sister tightening ever so slightly.

'Does she have any dietary requirements?'

'Well, we're vegan but she has formula milk when . . . Sorry, what does this have to do with anything?' Mum asked, blinking rapidly.

Sergeant Mistle stood, calmly placed her clipboard on the seat behind her then held her arms out. 'We'll need to know these things, so we can raise her effectively.' She looked straight at Mum. 'Hand over the baby, Miss Hall. We'll take her from here.'

Seven

Mum did a lot of swearing at that point. Most of it was about Sergeant Mistle wanting to be given Yula, but some of it was about the fact that it was *Doctor* Hall, not *Miss* Hall. Will gently picked up Yula and covered her ears as Mum exploded at the strange visitor, whilst Nick gazed at Mum, looking proud.

When Mum finally paused for breath, Sergeant Mistle clicked her pen authoritatively. '*Doctor* Hall,' she said, with the tone of someone who's discovered a slug in their breakfast cereal, 'Yula is no ordinary baby. She is what we call a Santa Baby – a Descendant who will one day grow up to become one of the most recognisable figures on earth. She will be a Claus, and that is to be celebrated.'

'I don't care if she's going to grow up to be queen of the entire universe,' Mum snapped. 'Right now, she's a baby. She's my baby. *Our* baby. She belongs at home, with people who love her.'

'But she has already caused alarm by doing magic in front of Unawares,' Mistle pointed out.

'Unawares?' I asked. I could definitely hear the capital letter in Sergeant Mistle's voice again.

'People who don't know the truth,' Nick explained. 'The truth about me, magic and Christmas.'

'Yes, sir!' Sergeant Mistle saluted yet again, nearly hitting herself in the eye with her pen. 'And as a dedicated member of the Elf and Safety Department, it is my duty to contain any magical mishaps and ensure there is no repeat of Unawares being alerted to magic.'

Nick took in a very deep breath through his nose. I recognised that sort of breath. It was the kind Mum did before she delivered a threat through gritted teeth. 'I understand your duties, Sergeant, but the matter is not up for discussion. Yula,' he said extremely calmly, 'will not be going with you. She belongs here. That's final.'

'But sir—'

'Are you honestly going to stand there and argue with me?' Nick stood up, pushing himself off the sofa in a way that made everyone in the room extremely aware of the fact that he was the real, bona fide and here-in-this-house Father Christmas. He wasn't frightening, not even slightly, but he radiated a sort of ancient power that seemed to make the very air crackle. He folded his tattooed arms over his broad chest. 'You really think you have a right to take my child, against my wishes?'

Sergeant Mistle looked up at him, duty and fury doing

battle on her face. Then righteousness won out, and her little cat's-bottom mouth pinched even tighter before she forced out two words: 'Yes. Sir.'

Nick actually looked somewhat taken aback. 'You . . . you do?'

Sergeant Mistle pulled a piece of paper from the collection on her clipboard. 'There is a precedent, sir. Back in 1883, after the eruption of Krakatoa, the Elf and Safety Department made the decision to suspend aerial deliveries. The Claus at the time argued against it and attempted to go out anyway, and eventually, to stop him, we had to impound the reindeer. Not a very merry Christmas at all. The Elf and Safety Department can override the wishes of the current Claus when there is sufficient evidence to—'

Nick took the paper and scanned it briefly, his dark blue eyes flicking back and forth as if hunting for a way out. When he lowered the page, he didn't look defeated, just annoyed. 'Let's not be hasty. I'm sure we can come to some sort of agreement. I can teach her to control her magic.'

'And how long will that take?' Mistle sniffed through her nose, looking pointedly at Yula who was now trying to eat her own hand. 'Elf and Safety. directives state – under paragraph 56, sub-section 904 – that any magic witnessed by Unaware human adults must be assigned a logical explanation by the Festive Imagination Bureaus. If a logical explanation, or F.I.B., cannot be provided, the incident will be deemed to be outside our control. What sort of logical explanation can be provided for a baby creating her own personal snow cloud?! I don't think I need to remind you that the foundation of Christmas magic is *believing*, not *seeing*. Unexplained magical acts could jeopardise the entire holiday!'

'In other words,' Nick said, thunderously, 'if Yula is spotted doing magic by an adult, and we can't come up with a reasonable explanation, she could bring about the end of Christmas?'

'Exactly, sir!' said Mistle, looking very pleased Nick had understood. 'Therefore, the recommended course of action is for the child known as Yula Hall to grow up at Claus HQ, in Lapland, where there's no risk of any Unawares seeing anything they shouldn't.' She stared at our stunned faces. 'You could always visit,' she added with a shrug.

Mum stood up, and for a moment she looked even taller than Nick. 'We didn't even know Yula was a Santa Baby until today! This is completely unfair! You have to give Nick a chance to teach her,' she said, in a tone which didn't sound like a request, it sounded like an order.

Sergeant Mistle, who had looked Father Christmas in the face and defied him, went pale under Mum's freezing stare. She glanced back at her clipboard. 'Well . . .' she squeaked.

'We're really good at secrets!' I said quickly. 'We'll make sure no one figures it out, even while she's learning. We've never told anyone about Nick, and we'd never tell anyone about Yula, either.' I looked at my sister. She was biting on a set of plastic car keys and smiling, oblivious to the fact her future was being discussed. Will was holding on to her tight, an expression of quiet determination on his face.

Sergeant Mistle fiddled with her pen, and her eyes flicked to Mum's steely expression once more. 'You get three strikes,' she said at last. 'That's how it works with you humans, isn't it? One practice, one mistake and one last chance. If Yula Hall is spotted doing magic this Christmas by an Unaware person, without a reasonable F.I.B. provided, I shall make a strike on my record. Three of those . . . and she comes back to Claus HQ with me.' Sergeant Mistle straightened up and slid her clipboard under one arm, before giving a salute to Nick.

59

We stood there, stunned into silence. This couldn't be happening . . .

Mistle saluted again. 'I'll be watching,' she said. And before anyone could say a word, she disappeared in a flurry of snowflakes.

Eight

'They won't watch her forever,' Nick said later that evening as he stirred an enormous vat of soup on the stove. It was just me and him in the kitchen, Mum and Will were watching Yula as she pulled herself up on the furniture and tried to stand by herself. I got the feeling Nick was cooking simply to give himself something to do other than worry. 'It's always hyper-vigilance during the Christmas season, and then they'll relax. They always get jumpy this time of year.'

'But how can we stop it happening?' I asked, worry

gnawing at my insides. 'Yula doesn't know she's doing it, does she?'

'Of course she doesn't!. And even as an adult, you can't control it entirely,' he said. He gave me a tiny smile. 'Not everyone transforms hot water into cocoa by accident, do they?'

I had to smile back. Nick's accidental magic was almost as fun as the stuff he did on purpose. 'So when can we teach her to hide it?'

'To be honest, the main thing we can do now is damage limitation,' Nick said, lifting his soup spoon to take a taste. He nodded to himself and turned the heat down. 'Minimise interaction with outsiders during Christmas where we can. We'll take her out of childcare for a while. She can come to work with me. And when she's older, I can show her how to hide her magic, or use it when it's appropriate. I know what it's like to grow up . . . like her.'

I watched Nick get some bowls out of the cupboard and tried to imagine him as a small boy. It seemed impossible that he'd ever been anything other than a big strapping man with a huge grey-white beard. 'Did *you* grow up at the Santa HQ?' I asked.

He gave a sigh as if the memory was complicated. 'Not full time,' he said. 'But I went there every Christmas season from when I was about your age, to learn the ropes. My great-uncle was the Claus before me. He still does some reindeer management back in Finland.'

I tried to work out how old Nick's great-uncle must be. But I had no idea how old Nick was either! He must have noticed my maths-face, because he chuckled a soft *ho ho ho*.

'You're the Claus for as long as you need to be,' he smiled through his beard at me. 'Your time can be brief, or last for eons. When it's time for you to retire, you just know it. And then you go back to living an ordinary life.'

'So . . . time doesn't work for you in the same way as it does for us?' I asked.

'No, not really. When you're Father Christmas, it's the biggest thing in your life. But this last year and a bit . . . being with your mum, and you and Will . . .' Nick switched off his soup pot and gave an affectionate stare around at our tiny kitchen. 'It's been good to remember just how magical the small things are, and how living an ordinary life can be so special.'

I got some bread out whilst Nick ladled the soup into four bowls and got one of Yula's baby dinners out of the fridge to heat up. It was so *ordinary*. Once again, I had to wonder how Mum had thought any of this could possibly work. But, it turned out, if you loved someone, you could make a lot of seemingly impossible things work, quite easily.

We all loved Yula, more than anything. Hiding her magic might seem impossible, but if Father Christmas could be my sort-of stepdad . . . I was beginning to believe that keeping baby Yula's magic secret was possible too.

*

Henry, Will's best friend, came over after dinner. The two of them were training for another PuzzoCube contest. This time, it involved working in a pair to solve identical problems on the puzzle cards. Will kept his treasured PuzzoCube on a velvet cushion. Henry's was a battered version of Will's, and it was a Christmas miracle he'd been able to get hold of one at all. Maybe an *actual* miracle, since no one in either family had been able to find one until Nick mysteriously came across it in an old shoebox at a car boot sale.

Nick could find a special toy *anywhere*.

'Hey Harper,' Henry said as he took his shoes off. 'You alright?'

I shrugged. I never knew what to say to Henry these days, having known him since he was six, but now he was nearly six feet tall and had a tiny moustache and he felt like a stranger.

'Hello, Henry,' Mum said, coming in with Yula, who was quacking like a duck and protesting to be put down. 'Sorry about the noise, she's tired.'

'That's OK. Hey, duckie.' Henry shook Yula's bare foot like it was a hand, which surprised her so much she stopped squawking.

'You're magic,' Mum said with a laugh. 'Will's in the dining room.'

'Thanks.' Henry went through, and just at the moment his back was turned, Yula waved her hands and snow began to fall from her fingertips.

'No, no, no,' Mum whispered urgently, putting her hand over both of Yula's. 'No, lovely, not here.'

Yula glared at her. 'Mamama?' she babbled.

'Sorry, sweetheart,' Mum kissed her head. 'No snow indoors please.'

Yula waved her hands again, but this time no snow came out.

'Good girl.' Mum kissed her again.

Yula was looking at her hands with a puzzled baby expression.

I went through into the dining room, where Will and Henry were working on their cubes with intense concentration. Nick was holding a stopwatch.

'Time,' he called, pressing the stop button, and the boys groaned, defeated again.

Henry ruffled his hair until it all stuck up like a hedgehog's bristles. 'This is *impossible*, William.'

'It's not my fault you're so slow,' Will said, but without any malice as he stared at his own failed puzzle. 'Maybe we should try those hand-strengthening exercises again.'

'Or maybe we should give up,' Henry said, head on the table.

'Shall I make you both a hot chocolate?' Nick suggested.

'Please!' Henry brightened, lifting his head up. 'You know, I reckon he's got to be some sort of hot chocolate chef,' he said to Will as Nick went into the kitchen. 'I've never known anyone make cocoa taste like you're drinking an actual chocolate bar, before. Your dad's a legend.'

I opened my mouth to point out that even if Nick was a suspiciously talented chocolatier, he wasn't our dad. But Will got there first.

'Yeah,' he said. 'He is.'

I stared at my brother.

Henry carried on, oblivious to my shock. 'I'm telling you, if *my* dad made stuff like that, I'd never leave the kitchen. They'd have to extract me with a crowbar.'

'He *has* shown me how he does it,' Will said, continuing to roll with the *dad* label. 'But it never turns out as good. Don't know why, must be magic . . .' He saw me staring and winked.

I didn't smile back. I turned and went upstairs to my

68

bedroom, my mind suddenly full of thoughts as uncomfortable as walking on pine needles barefoot.

A lot had changed since Nick had come into our lives. It had always been just the three of us – me, Will and Mum. When Nick and Mum started dating, I had been worried where he'd fit at first, but he had settled into our family perfectly and made it bigger and happier. But he was always just . . . Nick to me. A sort-of stepfather. Nothing else.

But now it appeared that Will thought of Nick as his dad.

The question was . . . why didn't I?

Nine

Will and me didn't see much of Yula that following week, because we were at school. And Mum had to go into work early each morning and came home late – apparently there were a lot of dogs who ate things they shouldn't during the Christmas season. And with the childminder's out of the question, most of the Yula-watching was left to Nick . . .

'I don't know what I'm doing,' he said morosely, one afternoon when I got home. Will had gone straight to Henry's house, and I'd walked into the kitchen to find half-mixed bowls of cookie dough on the counter, piles of laundry stacked haphazardly next to the baking ingredients, the oven on (cooking nothing) and a tray of unbaked gingerbread people in the fridge. Yula was sitting in her highchair, bawling her eyes out, red in the face. Nick looked ready to join her.

'Tough day?' I asked, surveying the carnage.

'A little bit.' Nick looked about. 'And she hasn't even done anything magical. She's just been a baby.'

Yula paused in her crying to take an enormous breath, before starting again.

'Is she tired?' I went over to her, and she swatted at me irritably.

'No. And she's not hungry, or wet or cold either.' Nick sighed. His longish grey-white hair was escaping from the bun at the back of his head as if he'd been pulling at it in frustration.

I guessed that Yula was probably thinking we were

both being really stupid. It must be terrible being a baby, unable to make people understand you. I stroked her head and gently picked her up. The change in location made her pause, but only for a moment before she started wailing again.

'Put those gingerbread people in the oven,' I suggested. 'I'll take her for a walk round the garden while they cook.'

Nick looked as though I'd promised him the moon and began tidying up quickly as I took Yula outside. The blast of cold air shocked her silent, and I let her gape at the coolness for a few seconds before pulling her hat on. She was so surprised to be outside that she didn't even try to pull it off.

'Better?' I asked her. 'Come on, you're driving your dad spare.'

'Dadadadadaa,' she replied.

'Yes, him.' I walked her out into the garden. Nick had

put up a swing set for Yula when she was born, and I plopped her into the plastic seat, giving her a little push. Like most babies, she didn't laugh or look happy, just stared in bewilderment as the swing rocked back and forth.

It felt ridiculous to think she was going to grow up to be a Claus. What did that even mean? Was she going to be Mother Christmas? Was she going to wear Nick's suit – that rugged red-brown outfit made of reindeer skin and fur? Was she going to have her own team of reindeer, with new names? Was she going to live in Lapland at Claus HQ, far away from an ordinary life?

Was she going to want to know us any more when she grew up?

I tried to push that thought aside, but the worries were very loud. Would Yula be able to quit being Santa Claus if she wanted to?

There were too many mysteries, and I didn't like them.

'Ba?' Yula said, as the swing came to a stop. Her face was no longer as red as a tomato, and she seemed to have forgotten about whatever was bothering her before.

I looked to see if she wanted another push, but she held her arms up instead, so I picked her up and kissed her on the hat. 'You've no idea how much trouble you've caused, have you?'

She made a happy noise and kicked her legs energetically. I lifted her into my arms, and a flurry of snowflakes lifted with her from the seat of the swing. They were gone in an instant, melted by the breeze, but it was enough to make me worry again.

When we went back inside, the kitchen was already much tidier and the place smelled deliciously of gingerbread baking in the oven.

Nick, however, was nowhere to be seen.

I glanced about, wondering if he'd gone upstairs for

a moment, when he came back through from the dining room, looking at something small in his hand.

'She's feeling better now,' I said, holding Yula up.

Nick jumped, not expecting us. He quickly put his hands behind his back. 'Oh, I didn't hear you come back in,' he said quickly.

'Yula's fine now,' I said. 'And the gingerbread smells great, by the way.'

'Oh yes, I'll just . . .' Nick made to sidle past me, his hands still behind his back.

Yula started to pull her hat off. I helped her with it, and by the time I looked back, Nick had his hands in the oven gloves and was taking the biscuits out.

Whatever he had been hiding was gone.

'Perfect!' he declared, tipping the tray so the little gingerbread people slid on to the cooling rack one after the other. Yula squealed and reached for them. 'Not yet, sweetheart,' he told her firmly. 'They're too hot.'

Yula screwed up her face, and I feared another enormous tantrum was on the way, but then she looked straight at the gingerbread people, and waved her hands.

'Are you saying bye-bye?' I asked her.

But she wasn't waving bye-bye.

The gingerbread people suddenly seemed to tremble on the cooling rack, steam rising from their little bodies, and then . . . *they sat up*.

I gasped.

Nick took a step backwards, and Yula laughed gleefully.

The gingerbread people slowly got to their gingerbread feet, looking about the kitchen with their little currant eyes. They lifted their gingerbread arms and scratched at their heads in confusion.

We all stared at them, Yula in delight, me in shock and Nick in absolute horror.

Slowly, Nick raised a hand towards them.

Immediately, the gingerbread people scattered. They

ran on their tiny biscuit legs at high speed, leaping off the counter and running about the kitchen, then dashing through the doorway to the rest of the house and sprinting towards the stairs.

'Catch them!' Nick yelled, as Yula squealed with joyful laughter.

Ten

To put it mildly, it was *pure pandemonium*.

The gingerbread people fled in all directions, diving out of sight like ninjas, doing commando-rolls through open doorways, sliding on their biscuity knees under obstacles.

Nick dived after them into the living room, where two were already attempting to scale the curtains. I swiftly put Yula into her highchair and grabbed the biscuit tin from the kitchen counter. I dumped the digestives out of it before rushing in to help – the tin had tall smooth sides, and I hoped the gingerbread people wouldn't be able to climb out of it in a hurry.

Nick grabbed the two on the curtains, one in each hand, and yelped as one of them pinched him hard between his finger and thumb. 'Ouch!' he gasped, dropping the gingerbread people into the biscuit tin. 'Good thinking, Harper. Leave the tin on the table, and let's try to find the others.'

'How many were there?' I asked.

'Fifteen,' he said, grimly. 'Two down, thirteen to go.' Inside the biscuit tin, the *living* gingerbread people crashed about and banged on the walls.

I put the lid on gently, just to be safe. 'Let's do this.'

The hunt was on.

I found my first cheeky biscuit sitting in one of Yula's plastic toy boats, waving cheerfully as it sat in a sink rapidly filling with water, the tap on full blast. I snatched it up and got it into the tin quickly before the water could melt it.

Nick appeared with two more clasped in his big hands, both of them struggling for freedom. 'They were under the living-room rug,' he said. 'Watch where you step!'

From her highchair in the hallway, Yula gave a shriek of delight – one of the gingerbread people was doing a tap-dance on her tray. I grabbed it and dropped it into the tin after Nick's. Yula howled in outrage.

The search continued. We emptied the waste-paper basket, combed through the Christmas tree branches, stopped one very daring gingerbread person from posting itself out of the letterbox, and found another in the fridge using a lettuce leaf as a blanket and a block of margarine as a pillow. There were two more having a fight on Will's bed, using a set of his knitting needles as weapons. I let Nick handle that situation and went into my room to find another one trying to squeeze itself between my Rainbow Catz graphic novels. I grabbed it and hurried downstairs, chucking it into the tin, just as Nick appeared with the two from Will's room.

'How many do we have?' I asked, sitting down and fanning myself with one of Mum's half-written Christmas cards.

Nick counted carefully, which was easier said than done as the gingerbread people kept climbing over each other and fighting inside the biscuit tin. 'Thirteen,' he said. 'There's still two missing.'

I looked around the living room in despair. There didn't seem to be anywhere else the biscuits could be hiding, short of underneath the floorboards. From the kitchen, Yula made squeaking noises until Nick went in and picked her up.

'I can't believe you did that, little miss,' he scolded tenderly.

'At least it was in the house, where no one else can see,' I said, starting to look behind the sofa cushions.

'True. This is just the sort of thing Sergeant Mistle

82

would count as a major strike if any Unawares were to catch sight . . .' Nick paused, listening. 'I think I can hear something scrabbling about . . .' He cocked his head and put a finger to his lips.

I went still and quiet, trying to listen. Nick was right. There was a little scratching-tapping noise . . . and it was coming from the kitchen.

At exactly that moment, Yula decided that it was too quiet and began to yell at the top of her voice, making us both jump.

'Quick – don't let them get away!' Nick cried, trying to shush Yula. I ran into the kitchen to see the two remaining gingerbread people scurrying out from inside the cereal cupboard and run across the worktop then leap heroically to the floor . . .

. . . just as the back door swung open and Will walked in, chatting to Henry and not paying the slightest bit of attention.

'NO!' I shouted, lunging forward.

Will looked down, saw the *living* gingerbread people scurrying about, and his face went white. He grabbed the first thing he could off the worktop – which happened to be a pair of Nick's neatly-folded underpants – and slapped it over Henry's eyes.

'What the—' Henry staggered backwards in surprise. The gingerbread people darted between the boys' school shoes, diving for safety.

I scrambled up off the floor, trying to run after them . . .

. . . but it was too late.

The two unruly biscuity figures sprinted down the garden, flung themselves into the hedge and disappeared from sight.

Eleven

It was not a good start to our 'Keep Yula's Powers A Secret' plan.

We were pretty sure that Henry hadn't seen anything (he did give a scream of horror when he realised what Will had clapped over his face, even though they were clean), but we knew it had been a close shave. Yula's magic had made gingerbread come to life. There was no telling what she might do next.

Will got Henry upstairs, and Nick and I sat in the dining room, looking down into the biscuit tin full of fighting figures. In all the excitement, Yula had fallen asleep and was now horizontal on her playmat, covered with a blanket.

'What are we going to do with them?' I asked. Two of the little biscuit people head-butted each other, crumbs spraying over the others.

'Well, we certainly can't eat them,' Nick said. 'Or throw them away. I shall send them to North Pole HQ. The elves will find a safe place for them in the workshops, give them something to keep them occupied.' He balanced the lid on the tin, put the tin into a box with plenty of air-holes and began taping the flaps shut. The gingerbread fighting sounds were muffled into near-silence.

*

Over the next couple of days, Nick kept watching Yula out the corner of his eye, as if worried she might bring other things to life, like the baubles on the tree, or the snowman-shaped sponges she played with in the bath, but our Santa Baby seemed content with playing just like any other baby.

We'd decided not to tell Mum about the gingerbread people, even though there were still two missing somewhere out there in the wilderness – she was so busy with work that we worried she might actually explode if she heard what had happened. We'd been on the lookout for the errant gingerbread people but had had no luck in finding them yet.

On the plus side, there was no sign of Sergeant Mistle. There had been no knocks at the door, no peeps through the window, nothing to indicate that she might be watching us.

'Maybe she's gone back to the North Pole,' Will said one evening, as we tried to get Yula to stand up without holding on to us. She was happy to pull herself up on the furniture and beam at her new height and was edging her way slowly towards the Christmas tree.

'Maybe she has,' I said but I wasn't sure I believed it. As always, I was right.

That Saturday was a day off for Mum, and Nick decided to treat us all by taking us to the Christmas market in the next town. It was bigger than our village, and the market square was packed with specially made wooden stalls, all selling festive wares. Wafts of spices and oranges drifted through the air, mixing with savoury bratwurst and yukky beer smells, and then finished off with a twang of candy floss and pretzels so sweet it made my jaw ache. The stalls were decorated with garlands of fake plastic greenery, interwoven with gleaming baubles and candy canes and flashing fairy lights. Steam billowed from cauldrons of hot chocolate and vats of soup, wisping over the paths that ran between the stalls. It was heavenly.

'Keep an eye on Yula,' Mum said softly as we walked between the stalls. 'There's a lot of people about – why did we think this was a good idea again?'

'Nothing's happened for days,' I pointed out. 'And Yula isn't the only one getting cabin fever.'

'Harper's right,' Will said. 'We need the fresh air, adults are always saying so. Besides, we're all watching Yula, aren't we?'

If Yula had any more eyes on her, she would have been a contact lens. But she was happily munching away, a massive pretzel rammed into her mouth. Yula was strapped to Nick's chest in her carrier, looking the very picture of innocence.

'Mum, can we have a go on the ring-toss?' Will asked. It was five throws for two pounds.

'Oh, those things are always rigged,' Mum sighed but got her purse out anyway and found a two-pound coin, which would give me and Will two throws each, with an extra go for Yula.

Will twirled his hoops around with a lot of bravado, before flinging them at the target. The first ring hit the target and bounced off, straight on to the floor, but, to everyone's surprise, the second one landed square on a peg just on the outside of the target.

The man running the stall did a double-take and looked closely at the ring and then at Will, who grinned. The man begrudgingly took down one of the smallest prizes – a bag of chocolate coins – and handed it over. 'Well done,' he sniffed. Will gave a sort of joyful cackle and started ripping the bag open.

'My turn,' I said. I half-hoped Nick might lend me some of his Christmas magic for a win, but right then he was preoccupied with Yula, who was gazing at the prizes with her big round eyes and grabbing tight to the plastic ring in her fists.

I threw my first ring and could tell by the way it spun that it was going to go wildly to the left. But the ring suddenly curved around in the air and landed neatly on a peg on the edge of the target, just like Will's.

'Oh,' I said, too surprised to say anything else as everyone turned to look at me.

'Mad skills,' a kid next to me said.

The man on the stall handed me a packet of sweets, his eyes narrowed in suspicion.

I looked at the second ring in my hand. It was a perfectly ordinary plastic ring but maybe it had a Frisbee effect when it was thrown. I decided to risk it.

I tossed the ring wildly to the right. There was no way it was going to hit the target – it would be lucky to stay in the stall. But, once again, the ring curved round and this time landed on a peg even closer to the middle.

The kids around me cheered, and the man running the stall went bright purple in the face, but there was nothing he could do other than hand me a second prize – a Make Your Own Giant Bauble kit.

'Next customer, please,' the man said gruffly, turning away.

But Yula babbled loudly and raised the ring she was holding, as if reminding him we still had one more turn. The people around us went *awwww*. The man pinched between his eyes. 'Fine, fine . . .' He gave Nick a stare. 'Throwing it for her, are you?'

Nick shook his head. 'No, no, not me.'

I breathed a sigh of relief. Nick was especially talented where Christmas games were concerned – he was likely to win the entire stall if he threw the ring! Yula, on the other hand, would more than likely just drop it on the floor.

'OK, little one, off you go . . .' the stall owner said, then stepped back.

Yula gave the ring in her hands a good stare. She looked at the target, and back at the ring, and then at me, and then back at the ring.

A nervous feeling coiled through my stomach. What if mine and Will's amazing throws were . . .

Before I could finish the thought, Yula flung the ring

with two hands. It sailed through the air, looping and spiralling, high and then low, spinning straight towards the middle of the board.

I looked at Nick and saw his eyes widen in panic.

The ring landed exactly square on the tiniest peg in the very centre of the target.

The crowd went wild. The Hall family did not.

Twelve

Yula's prize was an enormous stuffed toy dragon, almost as big as me. Nick had to cram it into a bin bag, hastily supplied by the very annoyed stallholder, and carry it over his shoulder as we shuffled red-faced away from the stall.

'That was fantastic! How did she do it?' people kept asking us as we tried to sidle quickly away.

We had no answer we could give them.. Yula had just done magic, right in front of everyone. And I felt certain that Sergeant Mistle would know what had happened. I kept expecting to see her beady little eyes and her pursed-up little cat's bum mouth around every corner. It was making me feel dreadful

Nick and Mum steered us all to a quieter corner of the market for a quick family meeting.

'OK, so that was magic, yes?' Mum whispered furiously.

'I'm afraid so,' Nick hissed back. 'Do you think anyone noticed?'

'Only the *entire world*,' Will said. 'And we don't exactly have a convincing F.I.B, do we?'

'Maybe she's been born with exceptional throwing skills?' I suggested, knowing even as I spoke that it sounded ridiculous.

The adults gave each other exasperated looks. Yula was gnawing on her pretzel again, oblivious to the fuss she had caused.

'Is this just going to be our lives at Christmas time from now on?' Mum sighed. 'Trying to hide our baby's magic powers and come up with a F.I.B to explain away her mistakes?!'

'I'm sure everything will be fine . . .' Nick said, in an entirely unconvincing tone. 'It was a slip-up, but now she has what she wants, I'm sure she won't do anything else.'

The un-talked about gingerbread people incident hung in the air between us like a bad smell.

Mum was no fool. She looked at our guilty faces and used her parent-powers to make a very quick deduction. She folded her arms and glared. 'OK, what haven't you told—'

'Ahem! Strike one!'

We all turned to see Sergeant Mistle standing in the middle of the path, holding her clipboard. Her conical hair was bright pink today, her suit and tie and splintery shoes a matching shade. Her tight little mouth was twisted into a sort of smirk, and her eyes glittered. The people walking through the market didn't seem to notice she was there – they walked around her like she was a bollard, and I guessed she was using some sort of magic to remain invisible to everyone except us.

'Strike one,' she repeated. 'A low-level magical disturbance that was perceived by several children and one adult, with no reasonable explanation. You promised to—'

'Alright, alright,' Nick said, holding his big hands up. 'It was an accident. Just the one time.' His words seemed to carry a lot of weight, and me and Will kept our mouths tightly shut.

Sergeant Mistle sniffed and wrote something on her clipboard. 'I suggest you work harder on maintaining your secrecy – Christmas isn't over . . . yet.' And with a last twist of her mouth, she vanished from sight.

We all let out a collective breath.

Yula dropped her gnawed pretzel on to the ground and clapped at it.

*

We might have made it out of the festive market unscathed, if it hadn't been for Mr Tipling. We'd been making a concerted effort to enjoy ourselves, trying some German biscuits and sharing a thick and gloopy hot chocolate that was nearly as nice as the kind Nick made. Mum bought a lot of little trinkets as presents, and Will found a ball of sparkly Christmas knitting wool. All of the shopping went into the sturdy bin bag Nick had slung over his shoulder, along with Yula's dragon.

We were just headed back to the car park, when a cry of joy came from behind us, making us all turn. Mr Tipling was trotting over to us, his face lit up from the inside like he was part reading-lamp. 'Oh!' he called. 'Oh, I say!'

'Do people actually still say, *I say*?' Will muttered.

Mum and Nick gave Mr Tipling equally wan smiles of tolerance. 'Afternoon,' Nick said, keeping walking.

Mr Tipling didn't take the hint. He scurried around

in front of us, clasping his hands together in delight. 'Oh I *say*!' he repeated. 'Look at you! The red coat, the beard and even the sack – you're the perfect image of Christmas!'

Nick seemed to look at himself from the inside somehow, mentally going over his appearance. He lowered the bin bag from his shoulder slowly, as if embarrassed. 'Erm.'

Mr Tipling didn't notice. 'Look, Mr, er . . .'

'Nick.'

'Nick! Perfection again!' Mr Tipling looked as if all his birthdays and Christmases had come at once. 'Look here . . . you'll recall I mentioned our Christmas parade? Well, I have a favour to ask . . .' He actually batted his eyelashes a bit. 'Your reindeer. The animals you look after at Farmer Llama's Petting Zoo . . . Would they be available to take part in our parade?'

Nick looked rather surprised. 'The reindeer?'

'Don't worry, we wouldn't need them for long,' Mr Tipling said quickly. 'Only for the parade itself – the party is afterwards, and we'd let them go home before that. But think of how splendid they would look, walking with the bells and whistles on down the high street. Would certainly get people in the Christmassy mood and want to donate to charity!'

'They *would* look great,' Will said, before he could stop himself.

'Yes, my lad, quite right!' Mr Tipling gave him two thumbs up.

'Just a quick walk down the street?' Nick asked. 'Nothing more?'

'Nothing more! We're very keen on preventing any undue stress to animals.'

Nick looked wretched for a moment.

'It would make a wonderful experience for your children, too, I should wager?' Mr Tipling wheedled.

Will nudged Nick. 'It'll be OK? Won't it?'

Nick looked down at Will, and I saw him undergo a sort of internal wrangling. Then, he sighed. 'Alright,' he said. 'One walk of the reindeer down the high street.'

'Wonderful!' Mr Tipling clapped his hands again. He shook Nick's hand, Will's hand and then Yula's sticky one, as she was looking left out. 'I'll be in touch! They'll look splendid in the evening, all lit up and covered in bells! I thank you, sir!' He gave a cheery wave and turned to skip back down to the market.

Nick blanched. 'After – after sunset?' He coughed, but Mr Tipling was already out of earshot.

I put a hand to my mouth. During the day, Nick's reindeer were as ordinary as any other animal. But by the light of the stars . . .

'Well,' Mum said, in a vaguely detached way that meant she was slowly filling to the brim with panic, 'all we have to do now is make sure that your magical reindeer

102

don't suddenly take off flying during the Christmas parade.'

'Sergeant Mistle is going to *love* this,' Will said with a groan.

Thirteen

Something was bothering me, but it wasn't to do with Sergeant Mistle. It was Will, again. When Mr Tipling said 'your children', it seemed to me like Will had easily counted himself amongst Nick's children. But in my head, Nick only had one child and that was Yula. He was our sort-of stepfather, but that was it.

Wasn't it?

In the car ride home, Will sat in the front passenger seat and Nick drove. The two of them nattered away non-stop about everything, from Will's knitting practice to Henry and the upcoming PuzzoCube tournament. They bounced around in the conversation like a pair of basketballs in a trampoline park.

Yula was behind Nick in her car seat, pulling tissues out of a packet and tearing each of them into a snowflake-shape that Mum tiredly took away every time it happened. I was too busy listening to Will and Nick to concentrate on my sister.

I was trying to work out when Will had decided that Nick was more than just *Nick*. We'd never had a dad, either of us, and I'd never missed one. Mum and Nick weren't married and didn't seem to be making any plans to be, and as nice as it would be to have a big party, that didn't feel important. What was undeniable was the fact that Nick was going to be around for the foreseeable future – he was Yula's dad, and Mum's boyfriend, and my . . .

. . . my what?

*

'So you're fine with people calling Nick our dad?' I asked when we were back home.

Will was knitting his Christmas-jumper-to-be again, performing each stitch like it was a medical procedure. They were all very neat, but he was only adding a new row every half an hour. And sometimes he unravelled it again five minutes later.

'What?' he asked, not raising his eyes.

'When Henry talked about Nick and called him our dad. *Your dad*. You didn't say anything.'

Will counted under his breath, before looking up. 'Does it matter?' he asked.

'Well, yeah. It matters because . . . he's not.' It sounded a bit pathetic.

The sort of condescending look only older brothers can give was aimed in my direction. 'Wouldn't you like him to be?'

I just stared, not able to come up with answer.

Will shrugged. '*I'd* like him to be. He's funny and kind and makes Mum happy. He joins in with my hobbies and he listens to me. He's my baby sister's dad. I'd like him to be mine too.'

It made sense when he said it like that. As dads went, Nick was a great one to Yula already. And he was caring and fun and made time for us. So why couldn't I say that too?

'You don't have to feel the same way I do about stuff,' Will said, kindly. 'Or people.'

He was right, but for some reason it felt like I was missing out on something. Like Will had more of Nick than I did. 'I don't know what to think.'

'You're not supposed to *think* about it,' Will said, starting to slowly knit again. 'You're just supposed to feel it.'

I watched Will knit for a while, trying to organise my thoughts. Nothing would change in our family if I decided to give Nick the *dad* label, so why did it seem like such a big deal? Maybe it was because I'd never had a dad before, and now I seemed to have acquired one by accident – one who was truly one of a kind.

*

I was feeling a lot of things right then, but most of it was worry. Worry about Yula, worry about Nick, worry about Mum. Worry about those missing gingerbread people! Every time I thought about the two of them on the loose, my stomach turned into jelly. We already had one strike against our family – if Sergeant Mistle learnt there was a pair of living biscuits running wild in our neighbourhood . . . she might decide that each one of them counted as a strike and then we'd lose Yula for good. Why oh why had I let them slip out of the door? No, that wasn't right. Nick and me had caught all the others, it had just been bad timing with the last two, and now I was lying awake fretting about it.

It wasn't fair, I thought to myself, punching my pillow.

Yula was being treated like she was doing something wrong, when all she was really doing was trying make Christmas magical. That wasn't a bad thing, she just didn't understand. She would understand, one day. By next Christmas she'd probably have it under control. You shouldn't punish people just for being who they were.

And we still had two strikes remaining. We were going to be fine.

Probably.

Fourteen

After the Christmas market fiasco, we tried to come up with a plan to get us through the festive season without any more strikes.

Will suggested never leaving the house until January – after all, he said, we had the fridge and the PlayStation, what more did we need? – which made Mum have to go for a lie down to 'think things over', though when I peeped in at her later she was doing a lot of snoring as well as thinking.

To give Mum a few hours of peace and quiet after

Yula was put down to sleep, we went with Nick to give the reindeer their evening feed.

The farm park was decorated for Christmas, and this year it looked as though they'd found some extra money from somewhere because alongside the cardboard sleighs and sagging snowmen of years gone by, there were bright new lights, some realistic-looking baby reindeer and an animatronic Santa that waved and wriggled in a robotic manner right next to the gift shop.

Nick gave it a harrumph as we walked past, and I couldn't help smiling. The waving model Santa was neat as a new pin with its prim red and white clothes, fluffy brushed beard and white gloves, whereas Nick looked scruffy by comparison. Of course, he was only in his work clothes at the moment, but Will and I had seen him in his proper get-up – his Father Christmas uniform as it were – and it was nothing like this doll. It was rougher, tougher, more real than anything on a Christmas card or on TV. Nick's Father Christmas clothes were made to keep him warm as he flew through the winter night air, protecting him from wind and rain and snow.

I hoped we'd get to see him in it again this year.

The reindeer recognised us, and when we got to the pen they came trotting over, tossing their heads so the bells they wore jingled and jangled. Their hot breath fogged in the cold air.

There were eight reindeer, just like in the song, but they weren't called Dasher and Dancer or Donner and Blitzen – Nick's reindeer were the descendants of those legends from the Christmas carols and stories, and even though they were many generations removed, they'd still inherited the magic of those ancient animals. During the day, they were just like any other reindeer, but their magic came alive by the light of the stars, and that was when they were able to fly.

'They won't try to take to the skies during the parade,

will they?' Will asked, scratching Lightning's head. She was so friendly, she was more like a pet rather than a highly trained working animal.

'They've been taught to stay on the ground whilst they're in the paddock,' Nick said, unbolting the gate. 'But outside the farm park . . .' He trailed off, then shook his head as if to dislodge the thought. 'They're good girls, for the most part. They usually do what they're told.'

Will looked at me, and I pulled a face. The year we first met Nick, one of reindeer had ended up on the roof of our house!

'I mean, they *have* escaped before,' I said gently to Nick.

He bolted the gate behind himself. 'That was just Meteor being naughty.'

'What if she's naughty again?'

'What if they *all* are?' Will added. 'If Mistle sees that *they're* out of control as well, she might think both you and Yula can't control your Santa magic. What if . . .' He clutched at his hair. 'What if she says you have to move back to the North Pole for good too?'

'That won't happen,' Nick said firmly, putting a hand on Will's shoulder.

'How can you be sure? We didn't know she was going to come for Yula, did we?' Will let go of his hair but it stayed sticking up in blond handfuls.

Nick gave a sigh. 'You're right. It's not worth the risk. I'll have to tell Mr Tipling I've changed my mind,' he said. 'I'll tell him that the reindeer can't go out, for some reason. I'll make something up.'

'Father Christmas tells *lies*?' Will asked, in sarcastic glee.

'He doesn't do it with any enthusiasm,' Nick said, taking his shovel out of the wheelbarrow and digging it hard into the grass to lean on the handle. 'But in this instance, it's for the greater good.'

Amor, a reindeer with more brown fur than grey, nudged Lightning out of the way to get some scratches from Will. Amor was the only reindeer we hadn't seen fly yet. When she hurt her leg a few Christmases ago, luckily, Nick had found a last-minute replacement for her.

A throaty 'baahhh' from the paddock behind us made me and Will jump. A llama with whiteish fur and prominent front teeth was watching us intently.

'Oh, it's you,' I said, picking my way carefully over to it. I was a bit wary of the llama. It was oddly very cute, but at the same time had a wicked look in its eye that seemed to suggest it might well be up to no good. I dreaded to think who was naughtier – the llama or Meteor. Still, the llama *had* come in handy a few Christmasses ago, when the team of reindeer needed an extra animal to help pull the sleigh . . .

'Do you think everything will be alright?' Will asked me, looking from the troublesome llama to the reindeer, then to Nick, who was now scooping reindeer poop at the other end of the paddock out of earshot. 'I really hope Nick can sort everything out. This all sounds like a great big soup of trouble.'

'It does,' I agreed. 'But remember what Mum says – if it's not alright, it's not the end.'

Will snorted then glanced up at me. 'You thought any more about the "dad" thing?' he asked, lowering his voice even further.

'No,' I said softly. 'It's too big to think about. It's like looking at the sun.'

'That's fair. Hey – imagine if they did get married, though.' Will nudged me.

'Mum would be Mrs Claus,' I said with a grin.

'As if. She'd never give up her own name. Even Yula is a Hall.'

'It would be great to have a big celebration, I think,' I said, thoughtfully. 'But weddings are expensive.'

'Yeah, but they could have it at North Pole HQ! How awesome would that be?'

I laughed. 'A wintry wedding . . . Mum could wear those welly boots she wears to work, and Nick could wear his Santa suit.'

Will clicked his tongue. 'Absolutely not, I'd make sure he had a top hat and a fancy suit at the very least. And we could have ice sculptures down the aisle, and reindeer . . .'

I narrowed my eyes at him. 'Are you thinking of getting into wedding planning next?'

'Ha, OK, you caught me,' he smiled. 'I do think I'd plan the heck out of a party, actually. All I need is the right opportunity.'

'Stick to the knitting,' I advised, as Nick shovelled up another huge pile of poo.

Fifteen

Tipling's World of Tipples wasn't so much a world as a small shop that shared an entranceway with the Turkish barbershop next door. The windows, always spotlessly clean, were full of fancy wooden displays of wine bottles, brightly coloured fizzy drinks from America, cans with cartoon characters on them and dark brown beer bottles with labels covered in unreadably elegant script. Since it was Christmas time, there were also fairy lights, miniature Christmas trees and fake snow in the window display.

It was one of those shops that never seemed to have anyone in it, and yet had been on the high street forever, somehow existing without a single customer. I knew Mr Tipling had to sell things sometimes (he changed his displays too often not to) but I'd never seen anyone enter or exit his shop.

A bell – a brass one that clanged rather than jingled – made a racket as Nick and I went in through the door. The inside of the shop was just as polished as the outside, with fancy tables covered in bottles and lots of tiny boxes of chocolates that didn't seem to have a price. If you had to ask, you couldn't afford it.

Mr Tipling looked up from behind his counter, where he was doing a crossword. His face lit up as he saw who it was. 'I say! Good afternoon, sir! What can I do for you?'

'I wanted to talk to you about the parade, Mr Tipling,' Nick said, getting straight to it.

'Oh, so do I,' Mr Tipling said, opening a drawer.

120

'Everyone is so excited about the prospect of reindeer leading the parade down the high street . . . even gruff old Mr Mann from the carpet shop said he'd come and watch. He's planning to donate five hundred pounds to our charity on Christmas Eve itself!' Mr Tipling produced a poster and held it out. 'We had these printed, look!'

Nick, his face frozen in a smile, took the poster and stared at it. It was a glossy full-colour image of some reindeer – not Nick's, but close enough – decorated with lights and bells with delighted children watching them. At the top it said, 'SANTA'S REINDEER ON PARADE', and below were all the details, reminding people to donate to the children's hospital charity.

'People are very enthusiastic this year,' Mr Tipling said, apparently not noticing how Nick had turned into a statue. 'It's so hard to encourage donations, especially when it's the same parade every year, but the reindeer have really added some zing! We should be able to raise enough money to buy every child in the hospital a wonderful Christmas present.'

Nick nodded, weakly. I knew he was quickly going through the excuses he had come up with and realising none of them was strong enough. He was Father Christmas . . . no matter how many worries he had about keeping the magic of Christmas secret, he was never going to let children down.

'Oh, listen to me, babbling on! You wanted to talk to me about the parade?' Mr Tipling asked, innocently.

'Yes,' Nick said slowly. 'I was wondering . . . what time it starts, exactly? Nice and early?' he asked, clearly hoping the beginning of the parade might be by the light of the sun, rather than the stars. 'To keep things as calm as possible for the girls, you understand.'

'Oh, I'm quite prepared to work around you and the deer, my good man,' Mr Tipling said. 'We always set off just as the sun has gone down – a magical time of the evening!' He pointed to the poster, where 'PARADE BEGINS AT SUNSET' was written in block capitals at the bottom. 'The reindeer will certainly start things off with a bang. It's going to be simply marvellous!'

To this, Nick had nothing to say. The reindeer were going to be in public by starlight, and there was nothing he could do about it. 'Perfect,' he forced out. 'We'll be there with bells on.'

'Wonderful!' Mr Tipling beamed. 'I just know we're going to smash our fundraising record and give all those children an unforgettable Christmas!'

*

By the time we got home, Will had added the start of an arm to his Christmas sweater. Well, a shoulder at least. It was extremely skinny. You might have been able to slip a strand of spaghetti down it, if you tried very hard.

'How did it go?' he asked us as we headed into the kitchen.

Nick gave a sort of resigned groan and covered his face with his hands.

'The reindeer are still in the Christmas Eve parade,' I said.

'Oh.' Will lowered his needles. 'Well, if it helps, Yula has been perfectly non-magical and well behaved all afternoon.'

'For once,' Mum added coming in. She carried Yula to our large kitchen sink, which was full of bubbles, and put her into it. Yula was wearing a baby-sized wetsuit and squealed happily. She loved playing with water. She picked up a tiny teapot we kept on the counter for her and started pouring the water out on to her hand, watching it intensely.

'If I give them all a good talking to before we start, and walk briskly,' Nick was saying, 'we might get away

124

with it. It's only along the high street, and then we can head straight back to the farm park. Then I can get the reindeer hitched up for deliveries later that night.' He looked at Mum, for her approval.

'I trust you,' Mum said. 'If you think you're capable of controlling them – they're good animals, they'll listen. Honestly, we have enough to worry about here. Yula, don't do that,' she added as Yula knocked the tap handle upwards to make the water pour out. 'The sink's plenty full.'

But Yula disagreed. She splashed her hands and a wave of water washed over the side of the sink and across the kitchen counter. As we watched, the water seemed to slow, falling to the floor in a solid curve that went stark white as it touched the lino.

Mum squeaked in disbelief as *solid ice* began to form on the kitchen floor. The tap continued to gush, and water was spilling out of the sink as the ice quickly spread, rushing towards the back door where it came to a stop. But not for long, as the ice quickly built up like an unstoppable glacier to shove the back door wide open, spilling the frozen water out into the garden.

Sixteen

The sheet of ice swept outside, freezing the ground under a solid layer that sparkled and glittered in the afternoon's mellow sunlight. In a matter of seconds, the whole garden had become weird sort of skating-rink, the ice coming to a stop only when it reached the fence, which was mercifully so high that the neighbours couldn't see over it. Inside, the ice covering the entire kitchen floor had pushed up right from under our shoes!

Yula clapped her hands in delight and scooted herself to the ice-slide she'd created from the counter-top to the floor, sliding down before anyone could stop her. She spun a little as she got to the bottom, cushioned by her padded swimming outfit. She seemed completely immune to the cold and held on to her bare feet laughing in sheer joy as she slid across the room.

Mum gasped, slipped forward and held on to the fridge door in panic. Will gave an experimental skid on his slippers, one hand still clutching his knitting. I wobbled crazily for a second before Nick caught me by the elbows. Yula was pushing herself back and forth across the kitchen ice rink as if this was all a wonderful game.

'Nobody move!' Mum was balanced like a star, arms straight out grabbing on to the fridge and legs in a triangle. 'Stay where you are!'

Will ignored this, using his slippers as ice-skates, gliding carefully over to Yula and giving her a high-five. 'Come on, Mum. Could be worse. At least this isn't in public.

You've got to admit that having your own private ice rink is pretty cool!'

'I suppose . . .' Mum stayed where she was, looking very uncertain as Will began to push Yula to and fro. I took a long look at my brother sliding about as Yula giggled uproariously – this was real *magic*! This was what I'd been imagining when we first realised Yula had powers. It was time for all of us to enjoy what she could do, instead of worrying about it.

I pushed myself off from the kitchen counter and skated out to join them. Will and I took it in turns pushing Yula across the ice as she shrieked with happiness. Nick was smiling as he took Mum's hand, watching us play, before Will gave the baby an unexpectedly big push. Yula slid straight across the room, over the slick frozen waterfall that ran down the step to the outside and shot out into the garden.

Will quickly skidded out after Yula, throwing his knitting on to the counter as he went, trying to keep his balance down the slick sheet of ice down on to where the grass ought to be. I awkwardly wobbled out after him, giggling.

Despite the frozen ground and ice, the air wasn't overly cold and everything seemed to sparkle with wintery magic. Yula had stopped in the middle of the garden and was laughing her head off, not bothered a single bit about the freezing ice – her cheeks weren't even red. A couple of very confused blackbirds were pecking at the ice, wondering where the soil and the worms had gone. Next-door's cat was patting the frozen ground in deep suspicion.

Will gave Yula a spin on the smooth surface. She went round and round like a pinwheel, laughing with glee, grabbing on to my trouser leg as she whirled past in a pink and blonde blur.

All our worries about Yula, Nick, Sergeant Mistle and

the North Pole seemed to melt away as we played outside. December so far had seemed to be one huge problem for our family, and it felt like we had almost forgotten how to have fun together. But this . . . this *was* fun. Properly fun. Just being outside with my brother and sister, Mum and Nick watching from the back door with their arms around each other . . . it felt so right. I wanted to freeze the moment and keep it safe, like we were all tiny figures in a magical snow globe.

*

As the sun went down, the Christmas lights in the houses around us flickered into life. The multicoloured glow shone through the air and on to the ice, which sparkled like a rainbow made of stained glass. The air rippled with colour and magic, and we skated about until it grew too cold to stay outside and Yula was starting to yawn. She let me pick her up and waved her arms absent-mindedly as I scootched carefully towards the back door.

The ice beneath us moved like a strange solid mass, inching its way out of the kitchen and down into the garden where it entered the pond and turned back into water, vanishing as if it had never been there at all.

Inside, the smell of cooking and spices greeted us. There were freshly made mugs of hot chocolate topped with cream and sprinkles on the counter-top. A pot of vegan chilli was stewing in the slow-cooker, and there was a big chocolate cake baking in the oven.

Will inhaled deeply and gave a smile. 'Things are alright sometimes, aren't they?'

'Yup,' I agreed, kissing Yula on the top of her sleepy head. 'Sometimes things are just perfect.'

But out of the corner of my eye, I saw a flash of something in the garden. As if a tiny person – or perhaps a person-shaped gingerbread biscuit – had run out of the bushes and sprinted across the garden and out of sight.

Seventeen

Playing in the icy back garden had been a nice reprieve from everything that was going on, but still, I was almost pleased to be going back to school the next day. At least at school there was nothing to worry about – no magic to cover up, no baby sister and no Father Christmas, at least. The worst that could happen at school was maths.

Nothing remarkable happened that day, until after lunch. We were in the hall for a drama lesson, learning about public speaking. It was my idea of a nightmare

– drama wasn't a horrible subject, but I was interested in working backstage rather than under the spotlights. Mr Beaumont, who taught drama across several schools and was more whirlwind than human, was focused on making sure everyone got to the front of the stage at least once. This term we were learning how to deliver a solo speech to a large audience.

Like I said, a nightmare.

We were taking it in turns to go to the front in groups and deliver a section of the chosen speech. The speech was not only boring, but also incredibly depressing – all about misery and bad times and spoilt meals and spilt milk. After listening to the first group, everyone was dissolving on to the floor, and there were five more groups to go. And my group was last. I began to wonder how I was going to survive the next hour.

'I swear this place has mice,' Rita Islam said from

where she was sprawled beside me on the floor. She shuddered. 'I keep hearing things scuttling about.'

'It could be giant spiders!' Tom Mackenzie said in what he thought was a menacing tone. He sounded more like he had a cold.

'Don't be weird,' Rita said. 'Listen.'

We all listened. And Rita was right – there was a scuttling noise coming from where everyone's bags and backpacks were piled up beside us.

'Urgh,' Tom said. 'I bet it's a rat trying to get into our lunchboxes!'

I'd been fine with the idea of mice, but none of us wanted to think about *rats*. Several people scooted out of the way, and others complained that they were never going to be able to pick their bags up again.

Ordinarily, I'd have been shifting out the way too, but my bag had my newest *Murder at the Tea-Party* book in it – *A Recipe for Revenge* – and I wasn't about to leave that behind to be eaten by rats or badgers or whatever else was lurking in the pile of bags and coats.

Gingerly, I pushed some of the bags aside and froze in shock. In the middle of the pile, holding a piece of leftover cheese and munching away on it, was . . .

. . . not a rat or a mouse, but *a gingerbread person.*

I nearly screamed. It was only surprise that stopped me. The gingerbread person looked up and gave me a cheery wave.

My first instinct was to clap a hand down on top of it, but I didn't want to risk crushing the escaped biscuit. I started to reach for it slowly as it watched me suspiciously.

'Is it a mouse?' Rita asked, making me jump.

My hand darted forward as I flinched, but the gingerbread person was quicker. It dropped the chunk of cheese it had been nibbling on and dived into the pile of bags, disappearing like a penny rolling down a drain. I plunged my hand in after it, up to the shoulder, scrabbling around to try and grab it somehow, but it was out of reach.

'It's a rat! It's rat!' Tom started dancing about and pointing and shouting as everyone else started panicking.

'It's not a rat!' I yelled. 'I'm not going to try and grab a rat, am I?!'

But the rest of the class were up and running around, shouting about rats and mice and weasels and ghosts and Bigfoot and whatever else might be hiding in the bags. Mr Beaumont waded into the mayhem to try to get everyone calmed down, but he was almost knocked over by the tidal wave of kids trying to grab their coats and bags and get away from whatever creature was roaming the hall.

By the time everyone settled down, the gingerbread person had disappeared completely. But I knew it was definitely somewhere in the hall. It must have crept back into the house and climbed into my school bag, and I'd brought it here without realising.

I couldn't concentrate for the rest of the lesson. My eyes kept flicking about the room, from the stage to the windows to the curtains and back again. There was no sign of any biscuity shenanigans . . .

. . . until it was my group's turn to do the speech.

I'd been so focused on the runaway gingerbread person, I hadn't even looked at the bit of the speech I was meant to be doing. I was the third reader out of five and was trying to pay attention to what Rita was saying, when I spotted it.

A small figure was climbing the blackout curtains at the back of the room, behind the rest of the class. My group were busy concentrating on the speeches in their hands and Mr Beaumont and the rest of the class were watching us, which meant I was the only person staring straight at the mountaineering biscuit, which had now climbed above head height.

There was nothing I could do! Tom was speaking now, right next to me, and I couldn't even hear him. The

138

gingerbread person was still climbing, a little cord of string around its waist like a safety device.

'Harper?' Mr Beaumont prompted. 'Your turn to read, please.'

My mouth flapped. I glanced down at the paper, but all the letters and words were swimming about and not making any sense. I looked back up. The gingerbread person was halfway up the curtain, and still going.

'Harper?'

'Sorry.' I looked back at the paper. I forced my mouth to start working. I have no idea how I managed to get through the speech.

But by the time I'd wobbled and wavered my way through the speech, and handed over to the next person, the gingerbread person had vanished over the curtain rail.

Eighteen

'It could still be at school,' I said to Will, later that afternoon. 'Or it could have snuck into someone else's bag and be anywhere in the village by now. And who knows *where* the second one is!'

Will's knitting needles clacked together as he listened to the story, sitting in the armchair like a wool-obsessed wise man. 'A gingerbread person on the loose in the school,' he mused. 'Interesting.' The jumper had one entire sleeve now. It was longer than the body by about fifteen centimetres.

'What are we going to do?' I asked. 'We need to find them!'

He shrugged. 'I don't see that we can do anything. Like you say, they could both be anywhere by now. Halfway to France, maybe. And besides, it isn't like Yula's ever been to our school, so no one will suspect she's anything to do with it.'

'And the other kids did seem to think it might be a mouse or something,' I said thoughtfully. Maybe there was nothing to worry about.

Will did something complicated to his wool, and then put his needles down. 'Gingerbread people aside, what are we going to do about the Christmas parade? Reindeer trotting down the high street? At night?'

'Don't.' I shook my head. 'It's going to be a disaster, isn't it?'

'Probably.' Will picked his needles back up and held the jumper between them. 'Does this look like it'll fit Yula?'

'Her leg, maybe.' I sat down on the arm of the chair. 'I don't know what's going to happen, Will.'

'Whatever happens, we're keeping Yula with us,' he said. 'We won't let anything happen to her. Ever.'

I nodded. 'Right.'

*

Mum had to do some Christmas shopping that afternoon and took us with her because she said she hadn't seen us for ages. That was true; with her work, school and all the Yula mayhem, we had been a bit of a scattered family lately. But even so, neither Will nor I enjoyed shopping for Christmas presents, especially not at the big new toy shop on the retail park. It was always too busy, too hot, and it was a special kind of torture to choose toys and presents for other people whilst coming out with nothing for ourselves. And then you felt guilty for wishing you had something for yourself!

It was Yula's first experience of all this, and after

ten seconds in the shop, she clearly agreed with me and Will.

'Ma!' she shouted, reaching for a box of colourful balls.

'No, sweetheart, they're not for you,' Mum said softly, patting her little hands.

'MA!' Yula insisted, her baby voice trying to shout *MINE*.

'Stinks, doesn't it?' Will said, giving Yula the shopping list to try and distract her. 'Seeing all the stuff you want but can't have?'

Yula frowned at the notepad and started banging it on the trolley in outrage.

'Let's move quickly,' Mum said. 'Before anything . . . happens.'

Even though it was a large one, the toy shop was horribly busy. I hated having to wear a big coat and then step into a warm shop: it was stifling in here, and I was soon sweating. Will was puffing out his cheeks and Yula was frowning so much that she looked exactly like an angry tomato. People were picking up books, jigsaws, dolls, teddies, and piling presents into their trolleys. Will spotted a 'teach yourself knitting' activity set and tried to point it out to Mum, but she was looking for a matching set of Princess Babies for our twin cousins and wasn't listening to him.

'Ma?' Yula tried hopefully, as the baby dolls were put in the trolley behind her.

'Not today, munchkin,' Mum said. 'If only they were one penny a doll, sweetie, but they're not.'

Yula sank down inside her coat, her already pink face going pinker, either from the heat or the annoyance.

'Not enough pennies!' Mum said, lifting up her purse and giving it a shake.

Yula probably didn't understand money, but she definitely knew that if anything came out of the purse, it meant a treat was on the cards. So when Mum put her purse back in her pocket instead of taking out any cash, Yula watched it disappear with suspicious blue eyes. Her little hands gripped the bar of the trolley tightly.

My stomach tensed. Oh no.

Not here . . .

I looked about the busy shop, chock-a-block with Christmas shoppers. If Yula did something magical here, there would be no hiding it, no way to come up with a reasonable F.I.B. I tried to pull Mum's sleeve, to get her attention, but we were so close to the tills that she was in Mum Mission Mode, trying to just pay and get out of there quickly. I clung to the metal of the trolley, ready to help get things scanned and packed as quickly as possible.

Yula turned around to look at the teenager who was working the till, scanning the contents of the trolley ahead of us. His face was screwed up in confusion. 'Sorry about this,' he said to the family waiting, 'I just need to check something . . .' He scanned another toy and then looked extremely worried. 'Erm, Kate?' he called across to the next checkout. 'My till is doing something weird.'

'Yeah, mine too,' the other cashier, called back. 'What shall we do?'

'What's going on?' Will asked softly.

Yula made a few sing-song noises and pointed at Mum's coat pocket.

Mum touched her purse. 'What on Earth?'

The family ahead of us were suddenly looking extremely excited. They were talking quickly together, pointing at the cash register as . . .

'Uh-oh,' I breathed.

'It's everything I scan,' the teenage cashier said loudly. 'It's all going through as one penny. Everything in the store is one penny!'

A silence dropped over the entire shop, as the message echoed down every aisle.

And then, it was complete and utter mayhem.

Nineteen

The till queue snaked through the shop, every single trolley piled high with stuff. Toys, games, puzzles, soft teddies, water pistols, games consoles, bikes, skateboards, paddling pools and computers were all being held on to tightly by astonished and gleeful shoppers.

'MA!' Yula squealed happily as Will picked up another Princess Baby doll set from the shelf and handed it to her.

'Seems we might have enough pennies after all,' he said softly.

'She did this, didn't she?' Mum whispered urgently, nodding her head in the direction of our trolley.

We looked at each other. Yula held up her doll and giggled. Around us the other shoppers were exclaiming delightedly, laughing in amazement at unexpectedly being able to afford anything they wanted. But it wasn't all Christmas-card joy and happiness. There was a lot of panic as well. People were snatching things off the shelves, grabbing bicycles and scooters by the handlebars and wheeling them towards the tills, elbowing each other and holding tight to their baskets and trolleys as if someone else might try to snatch them away. One dad had his kid laying on top of his full trolley, starfish-style, like a human security net.

No one was fighting but everyone's arms, baskets, trolleys and bags were filled to bursting with *stuff*, and everyone was looking at each other with suspicion, as if the shop was suddenly filled with thieves.

The staff in the toy shop had closed the entrance so no new customers could get in. The till operators were scanning through goods, trying not to be too frantic whilst calling across to each other as they tried to work out what had gone wrong with their systems.

Yula patted the box of her new doll and sang, 'Ma, ma, ma,' to herself.

Mine, mine, mine.

'Next please.' The teenager on the till called us forward.

Mum started putting the items on the conveyor belt. 'So strange this happened all of a sudden,' she said, her voice going high-pitched, the way it does when she's anxious. 'But I guess these things happen, the tills going wrong – must be a computer virus! Still, very Christmassy!'

'I guess it's no one's fault,' the cashier said, but he didn't look too happy. 'But I worry about all the shoppers who didn't make it to the store today – will there be any toys left for them to buy for Christmas?'

'Oh,' Mum said, realising as well. 'I didn't think of that . . . but won't you get more deliveries?'

'Not this late in December,' the cashier said unhappily. 'Once the shelves are empty, they won't be filled again before New Year. When these toys are gone, there'll be no toys left for anyone else this Christmas.'

I looked behind us beyond the huge queues of people. The shelves were nearly stripped bare. How many of the items stacked high in people's trolleys were actually on their wish lists? Or could people just not resist grabbing a skateboard for a penny? I imagined shoppers standing outside the locked doors, or turning up tomorrow – all of them coming to get presents for their families, only to find empty shelves with nothing left to buy, even at full price.

My heart felt like it was sinking right down through my body.

Yula looked up from her doll. Her happy little face

softened as she looked from the cashier to me, then to Mum. And then, to the empty shelves.

I patted her hand reassuringly. She hadn't meant to cause this scenario. She had just wanted to make it possible for her mum to buy her the toy she wanted. How could a baby predict what would have happened next?

Yula's blue eyes seemed to sparkle in the sharp overhead lights. She gazed steadily around at the bare shelves of the shop, and for a moment she looked much older than she was – just in the eyes. Ordinarily, Yula was the image of Mum – same as me and Will – with the blonde hair and a little snub nose. But right then, I saw her dad in her face – I saw Nick's magic in her expression.

She looked up at the bright overhead lights. At the empty shelves. And she raised a hand.

I gasped. 'Yula! Yula, don't—'

The lights went out.

A lot of people screamed, and for a second there was shouting and crashing.

But not a moment later, the lights came back on. Flickering and buzzing with that strange fizz and crackle of industrial lights, they popped one by one into life. First, the tills were lit up. Then, the waiting areas. Then, the aisles themselves were illuminated again . . .

. . . and the shelves were full. Not of toys, games and books – but boxes. Sealed-up packages with labels that said things like *Contents for tax purposes: Toys*, and *Express Delivery* and *Airmail* on them. Boxes full of new stock, ready to be sorted and put on the shelves.

They had appeared out of nowhere.

As if by magic.

'Oh, baby girl . . .' Mum murmured, stroking Yula's head, clearly at a loss for anything else to say.

Yula looked very pleased with herself.

The cashiers were looking at each other and shrugging,

pressing buttons on their tills as though that might put the world back to normal.

Yula clapped her hands, as if giving herself a round of applause, and Will had to hide a smile.

Still, the temporary blackout had put the other shoppers on edge. Everyone just wanted to pay and get out. We handed over the few pence we owed for our toys, and quickly pushed the trolley outside. The way in was still locked – I guessed the staff would close the store once the remaining shoppers were safely outside, and then work out what to do with their unexpected delivery.

'Magic,' Will said, sounding far away and breathless.

'Magic,' I agreed. My legs felt wobbly, and my hands were tight on the metal of the trolley. It was magic, in such a public place . . . there was no other explanation we could give. None at all. If anyone had spotted Yula raising her hands just before the blackout . . .

'It's going to be OK, isn't it?' Will asked.

'No one will think it was magic,' I said, not believing myself.

Yula cooed over her new doll, looking anything but magical as she tried to give the baby a kiss and ended up chewing on its face.

Mum wasn't saying anything. Her jaw was clenched and her hands were white on the trolley handle.

We made it all the way back to the car before Sergeant Mistle popped into sight. She stepped out from behind an impossibly skinny lamp-post, her high heels clicking over the pavement as she tottered towards us, her conical hair now red and white; swirled through like a candy cane.

'Strike two,' she said triumphantly. She tapped her clipboard with her pen and gave a disapproving glance at our loaded shopping trolley. 'One more mistake, and the Santa Baby is coming with me.'

'She just did that so everyone in the shop could afford the toys they wanted, and so everyone else would still be able to buy their presents too,' I hissed. I wanted to snatch the stupid clipboard out of her hands and snap it in half. 'She was being kind! She wanted to give people presents – isn't that what being Santa is about?'

Sergeant Mistle blinked in surprise, but regained her attitude quickly. 'It isn't that simple,' she said. 'She is jeopardising Christmas.'

'She doesn't understand that it's wrong!' I insisted.

'Leave Yula alone,' Will added. 'How can you be angry with a baby who wants to make people happy?'

'I am not angry with her,' Sergeant Mistle sniffed, in a tone that made it difficult to believe her. 'I am simply seeking to ensure the survival of Christmas as we know it. Free, or almost free, presents for everyone? Suddenly appearing toys? These are trademark Claus effects, recognised by children and adults all over the world. And no reasonable F.I.B. has been given to all those shoppers. *Someone* will suspect.'

'But they'll never suspect *her*!' I nearly shouted. 'Nick walks around with a white beard and a red coat on all day and manages to shrug off any suspicion – why would anyone think Yula was to blame?'

'You agreed to the terms of this arrangement!' Sergeant Mistle squeaked through her nose. 'One more mistake, one more public display of magic, and Yula Hall is coming back to the North Pole with me.' And with a flurry of snowflakes, she vanished.

*

Later, back home, we gathered in the living room for an emergency family meeting.

'Maybe it *is* safer for her in Lapland,' Mum said, but without much enthusiasm. 'We could go with her. We could all move up there, to the North Pole.'

'What?!' Will shouted, dropping his knitting.

The shopping was still in the back of the car, except for Yula's new doll, which she was now dunking head-first into a pot of yoghurt. Nick had made Mum a drink that was a bit stronger than hot chocolate and had listened to the story with a grave face.

'We can't go and live in Lapland,' I said. 'What about . . . school? And your work? And all our friends?'

'Well, what other choice is there?' Mum asked. 'We can't let them take her away. And we haven't been able to stop her doing magic, or provide good enough excuses when she does – and I don't see how we can. We should all go together. As a family.'

'But that means letting Sergeant Mistle win!' I insisted. I looked at Nick. 'We can't give up, can we?'

He gave me a smile through his beard, the twinkle in his eyes so like Yula's that I suddenly understood – it was the twinkle of Claus magic I had seen on Yula's face. It was the impossible, festive skill they both had, to bring joy and happiness, even if it didn't make sense. Even if it changed the world.

'It's not over yet,' he said. He put an arm around Mum. 'According to Mistle, we still have one more chance. And I promise you all, Yula is going nowhere.'

Twenty

It was Christmas Eve, the day of the Village Christmas Parade.

Mr Tipling had come to our house twice to check everything was still OK for the reindeer to take part, and the second time he even followed Nick and me and Will to the farm park, chatting non-stop about how wonderful real-life reindeer walking down the high street would be. Nick was trying his best to be polite, I knew, but his nervousness and frustrations over Sergeant Mistle and Yula were making him fold his arms a lot more than usual, and eventually he had to practically push Mr Tipling out of Farmer Llama's gates to get some breathing space.

'Four o'clock,' Nick said as cheerfully as he could manage through gritted teeth. 'We'll be there!'

'I'll leave you to your preparations then!' Mr Tipling called, as if he was doing us a big favour.

We breathed a sigh of shaky relief, but Mr Tipling wasn't the last of our concerns. Earlier, Mum had volunteered to stay at home with Yula to avoid any public displays of magic, but at the last second she was asked to go down to the vets' practice because someone's cat had stolen and eaten half a turkey and was now too full to walk. So baby Yula was with the three of us.

Nick had his official Father Christmas uniform hanging up in the securely-locked barn at Farmer Llama's, ready to put on as soon as he got back from the parade. The suit wasn't a lurid scarlet and fluffy stark white like those costumes we'd seen on the parade posters; Nick's suit was a hand-dyed brownish-red and made of reindeer hide, not polyester. The wrists and buttons were trimmed with thick brown reindeer fur, and the suit also comprised heavy braces, wind-proof goggles, a hefty belt, a hat and thick gloves to keep the cold wind at bay. It was a suit for Serious Santa Business.

Also in the barn was the sleigh, parked up and ready to be loaded with gifts. Like the suit, the sleigh was rough and stained, suitable for heavy use. Its enormous wooden body, the size of a lorry, sat on metal skis that curved upwards like blades, gleaming in the light. Shining new attachments had been bolted beneath, looking to me like silver tubes. The long seat at the front of the sleigh – wide enough to squeeze on four regular-sized adults – was fronted by a safety-bar of wood as thick as a tree-trunk, gnarled and carved with festive leaves. Greenery was woven through the gaps, holly and ivy shining within the reddish wood.

I touched the sleigh gently, as though it was alive. Very few people got to see this. The workers at the farm park had no idea it was there, and millions of sleeping children would be visited by this amazing thing, and never catch a glimpse of it. And Will and me had ridden on it! We were beyond lucky.

Nick caught me looking longingly and smiled. 'Fancy another trip tonight?'

My heart rose. Last year, with the rainstorm, there had been no chance of a trip. This year, the skies were cold and clear – perfect flying conditions. 'Definitely,' I said with a grin.

'Let's see how this parade goes, and maybe we can set off before it gets too cold,' he said. He looked worriedly at the empty cargo hold. 'It's going to be tight on time, getting back, loading up and taking off.'

'Doesn't time work differently for you on Christmas Eve?' Will asked. 'You do have to get all the way around the world after all.'

'As long as I can take off on time,' Nick said. 'It's been touch and go a few times in the past . . .'

'It'll be fine,' I said, though my stomach felt like it was full of snakes. 'Shall we go get the reindeer?'

We left the barn and went out to the paddock, where Will, Yula and the reindeer were waiting. Yula was proudly sitting on the back of Meteor, holding tight to her harness with Will's hands circled around Yula's middle.

'All set?' Will asked as he lifted Yula up, making her squeal as he spun her around.

Nick and I nodded. There was nothing else we could do but set off. The parade wouldn't start until we arrived.

Nick took up the reins at the front of the team of reindeer: Sprinter and Courser were first, side by side, followed by Starlet and Kit, Thunder and Lightning and finally Meteor and Amor at the back.

The stars were just glinting into life. The sky was fading from red to the darkest blue. It was showtime.

*

The village square was heavily decorated for the Christmas Eve Parade. Each tree had fairy lights wrapped around its trunk, and there were more in the branches. Every lamp-post was bedazzled with glow-in-the-dark angels and stars, and twinkling bulbs were suspended above the little tables and stalls selling biscuits, cakes, hot chocolates and mulled drinks. The clear darkening sky shone with stars, and delicious smells wafted across the air, but they did little to warm us as the temperature seemed to have suddenly dipped.

'It's f-f-freezing,' Will said from somewhere inside his massive scarf and thick parka. He had his gloved hands clutched tight on to Yula's pushchair. She was complaining loudly – she much preferred to be in the baby carrier where she could see what was happening, but Nick needed to concentrate on the reindeer, so me and Will were going to be babysitting until Mum managed to get away from work, or until it was time to walk back to the farm park. 'Please can we get this over with?'

'As quickly as possible,' Nick promised. He held firmly on to the front reins of the reindeer. The animals were snorting and moving about impatiently. It felt as though we'd been standing here for ages, waiting for Mr Tipling to tell us to set off down the street.

We were waiting so long in fact that finally Mum managed to join us. 'Have you not even set off yet?' she asked in disbelief.

'Yeah, we've been down the street once but fancied another go,' Will said, dripping in sarcasm fuelled by the cold. 'Are you only just finished with work?'

'Yes, it turned out to be a long job. I thought there

was a chance you might still be here.' She looked at Nick. 'I'll take the kids for a hot drink, and then get them home, they look frozen.'

'Of course. Save one for me,' Nick said, adjusting his grip on the reins as Sprinter tried to muscle up to Mum to say hello.

We peeled away into the crowd and headed over to the food stalls, grabbing some hot chocolates that weren't a patch on Nick's. These could be generously called 'hot brown water', and Mum balked at the price but had no choice but to pay up as Will had already swigged half of his.

'Let's drink these and head home,' she said, suddenly, as if she'd just made a snap decision. 'Nick will manage the reindeer just fine, and then he can quickly get them back to the farm. Besides, I don't like to think of what Yula might do in front of this crowd on the most magical night of the year,' she added in an undertone.

'But Nick said we could go flying with him, tonight!' I said, suddenly filled with misery at the idea of not being able to go *again*.

Mum hesitated. 'Oh love, I know he promised but . . .'

A bell suddenly rang, and we turned to see Mr Tipling, wearing an incredibly plush Santa suit, standing at the top of the road. The suit was a vivid red and pure white, and had clearly never seen a real day's work in its life.

'Ho ho ho!' he called in a warbling soprano. 'It's me! Santa Claus! Make way for my famous reindeer!'

There was a smattering of polite applause, which quickly rose and turned into genuine cheers as Nick led the eight reindeer slowly and calmly down the road. I had to admit, they looked amazing. Their decorative red harnesses shone in the fairy lights, and their jingling bells had been polished to a shine. Even the fuzziness of their antlers seemed to have a sheen as they stomped proudly past smiling children.

Mr Tipling skipped along, ringing his bell, his false beard riding up over his nose. He gave us a cheery wave, and we waved dutifully back. The reindeer were indeed the main attraction. They stopped to let children stroke their woolly noses and touch their antlers gently, and adults dropped a stream of coins and notes into charity buckets carried by Mr Tipling's 'elves' – actually a couple of teenagers from the local high school wearing jingly hats. The fundraising was going to be a great success.

I looked at Will and grinned. He smiled back.

Across from us, the choir started to sing. It was a wobbly sort of church carol I'd not heard before, but it was peaceful as a backdrop for the reindeer and the children. It felt almost magical, in fact. I had to suppress a laugh when I noticed that the choir was being conducted by the same woman who delivered our post – she looked a lot different in a fluffy Christmas jumper and with tinsel wrapped around her head.

'Let's hear it for Santa!' she called over the microphone, to more cheering. Will and me clapped hard, and Yula kicked her legs in the pushchair. 'Your generosity is much appreciated – let's not forget the true meaning of Christmas; sharing what we have, and helping others when we can.'

Coins rained down into the collecting buckets and I saw Nick breathe a sigh of relief. He gave the woman on stage a nod, and she winked back.

The choir continued to sing, changing from a church tune to something with more bounce, and the singers started to dance a little.

I was gazing at the choir when, down by their feet, I saw it.

A gingerbread person.

It was striding out from the crowd into the road, a tiny figure seemingly unseen by anyone else.

Heading right into the path of the reindeer's massive hooves.

171

I gasped and braced myself for the *crunch*.

But I wasn't the only person to have spotted it. In her pushchair, Yula went, 'Na!' and before anyone could react, she reached out both hands towards Starlet's stomping hooves. There was a sort of throb in the air, and to my absolute horror, Starlet stepped *on to* the air, the way she did when she was getting ready to fly. The gingerbread person, saved by the somehow solid pillow of air under Starlet's hoof, quickly scuttled back into the crowd, but by the time it had disappeared, Starlet's strange step had been noticed.

'What's wrong with that reindeer?' someone close by me asked. 'Is it hurt?'

Starlet seemed to be struggling to put her leg back down. She was causing a traffic jam, the other reindeer unable to move forward. Mum darted out into the road, straight over to Starlet, but I knew the reindeer wasn't injured – she had taken a single flying step, and now was stuck, one leg in flight, the other three trying to stay on the ground.

'Yula!' I hissed at her.

She was frowning and shaking her head. Starlet tried to step again, her front leg going even higher this time.

'It's like she's trying to fly,' someone else said, laughing. 'Hey – real reindeer that really fly, that would be worth seeing!'

The choir's singing stuttered, as if they were distracted, and I saw the conductor turn to look at the reindeer, genuine concern on her face.

'Oh, no . . .' Will turned the pushchair around, away from the parade. 'We need to get out of here!'

Mum was trying to get Starlet to put her leg down and Nick was coming forward to help, and Yula clearly didn't want to lose sight of either of them because she wailed loudly. Instantly, as if someone had cut them with

173

scissors, the reindeer's harnesses fell away, and dropped, jingling, on to the road.

The crowds took a step backwards. All of a sudden, the reindeer had gone from being a special festive treat to being large animals on the loose. Will and I carried on marching away, parking Yula's pushchair behind one of the stalls, where no one could see us.

Or so we thought.

'Strike three!' a wicked voice hissed from behind me.

I turned to see Sergeant Mistle, her hair and lipstick purple again, grinning smugly. 'She didn't do anything,' I lied desperately.

'How dare you lie to an Elf and Safety agent!' Sergeant Mistle gasped. 'That reindeer is struggling to stay grounded, and the others have been spontaneously released. I think we all know the culprit,' she said, looking meaningfully at Yula. She snapped her fingers and Starlet's leg dropped down to the ground with a *CLACK*.

'*And* a living gingerbread biscuit was spotted roaming the streets.'

'Spotted by whom?' Will demanded.

'By me,' she said. She snapped her fingers again, and the straps holding Yula into the pushchair burst apart. My sister floated up into the air and straight into Sergeant Mistle's arms.

Yula laughed as if the experience was a joke, but then squirmed, furious, as soon as Mistle got hold of her.

'Get off her!' I cried, but my feet seemed to be frozen to the pavement. Will, too, was struggling and reaching desperately for our baby sister but Mistle's magic had us frozen where we were.

'There will be a letter sent to your mother about future visiting arrangements,' Sergeant Mistle squeaked.

'We'll follow you!' Will shouted. 'You can't run from us!'

'I don't need to run,' Mistle grinned. She gave a whistle,

and a llama – *the* llama, the one from the farm park that had helped to pull the sleigh last year – trotted into view from behind another stall, a small sledge, like a shrunken version of Nick's impressive sleigh, tethered to its back. 'We shall fly.'

'And you think no one will notice?' I yelled.

'Oh, yes, I almost forgot we needed a distraction . . .' Sergeant Mistle looked back at the reindeer and snapped her fingers one more time.

The reindeer, as a group, reared up and roared as if someone had stuck a pin in each of their bottoms. The crowd began to move away quickly, afraid of the antlers, the hooves, the massive teeth . . . The reindeer's hooves struck sparks as they pawed the ground.

And then, they charged.

Twenty-one

Nothing scatters a crowd like eight charging reindeer.

Lightning clattered down the high street, head down, antlers leading the way like a battering ram. The bystanders parted instantly, everyone running for cover, not even looking back as they pelted for the safety of the shop doorways around them. And a good thing, too, because Lightning was quickly followed by Thunder, Amor and Starlet, all of them pounding the pavement with their hooves. Sparks flew, and the frightened yelps of the people were mingled with the deep throaty roars of the animals – they were on a mission, and nothing was going to stop them.

Sergeant Mistle leapt up into her sledge and thrashed the tethered llama with the reins. The llama gave a honk of shock and hauled itself into the sky quicker than blinking. Before I'd taken another breath, it was amongst the stars . . . and our Santa Baby with it.

'We have to *do* something!' I yelled to Will. Our boots were unstuck now, but I couldn't see Mum or Nick amongst the panicking crowds.

'Harper, come on!' Will grabbed my sleeve and pulled me forward, almost into the path of two of the reindeer. My life flashed before my eyes, but instead of crashing into us, Amor and Starlet skidded to a halt and made tossing motions with their heads, craning their necks back.

It didn't take a genius to work out what it was they wanted.

Climbing on to a reindeer's back isn't easy in the midst of a panicked stampede, but we managed it as quickly as we could. With a determined roar, Amor and Starlet took off again, Will and me clinging to their harnesses and fur. The reindeer were running so fast they seemed to be flying over the street . . .

. . . and then we really were *flying*.

The reindeer's hooves dug into the air itself like it was solid ground, and they hauled themselves up into the blackness of the sky . It happened so fast that one moment we were on the street and the next we were amongst the clouds. There was no way any of the frightened people below would have seen a thing. The reindeer were using magic of their own, that was for certain.

I clung on to Amor's reins so tightly my hands started to hurt in my gloves. The icy wind whipped at my face, and I was grateful I'd remembered to wear a hat and scarf because the snow clouds we were charging through bit and scratched at any exposed skin like needly teeth. Still, we were flying!

Beside me on Starlet, Will was shouting something and pointing. I couldn't make out what he was saying over the wind, but what he was pointing at was obvious – a very small sledge-like object not too far in the distance, being pulled by an animal with a long neck and fuzzy white fur.

'That's her!' I shouted to Amor.

Whether the reindeer understood me or not, I have no idea. But she seemed to find some extra strength from somewhere, and stormed forward through the dark with me hanging on to her neck for dear life. We were so high up now that I couldn't see the ground at all.

We raced after the llama-pulled sledge, but as fast as our reindeer ran, we didn't seem to be getting any closer. We were keeping pace, so they stayed in sight, but remained just out of reach.

Then, the air seemed to vibrate, and a heavy *whoooooosh* sound boomed around us that seemed to drag the wind downwards, and something big – something red, something *enormous* – flew into the air, right beside me and Will.

A sleigh – one we knew, one we had ridden in – pulled by the remaining six reindeer shone golden in the starlight. There were two figures in the front seat, both of them waving madly.

'Mum!' I yelled. 'Dad!'

Dad?

The sleigh swooped closer, and now it was airborne I could see the new modifications properly – the silver shapes were like cones, flared at the back and polished perfectly smooth. There was an orange glow coming from the flared bit, as if they were rockets ready to take off. Maybe they were! Two years ago, Nick had been worried about only having a team of seven to pull it. This year, whatever had been done to the sleigh had made it possible with just six.

'She's over there!' Will shouted, pointing. 'Straight ahead!'

Nick saluted, then touched something in the cab of his sleigh. The giant sleigh and reindeer seemed to suddenly rocket forwards, Nick and Mum leaning back against the force of the speed.

Me and Will whooped in delight. Our reindeer steeds, Starlet and Amor, tried their best to keep up, but the sleigh was zooming ahead, gaining on Mistle and the llama with determined speed. It drew level with the smaller sledge, and I could see Nick shouting and gesturing. Yula was just about visible, looking like a big ball of cotton wool strapped into a seat.

The Elf and Safety agent thrashed the reins on her llama, trying to pull away, but Nick was clearly having none of that. I watched as he handed his reins to Mum and edged to the very lip of the seat on the large sleigh. Hanging tight on to the sleigh's thick tree-trunk bumper with one hand, he reached out with the other, and made to grab at Sergeant Mistle's sledge.

'He's not going to make it!' I gasped. I had a terrible vision of Nick – of Father Christmas – slipping from his sleigh and falling down into the night with nothing to catch him. My heart clenched.

But I needn't have been worried.

Nick grasped once, twice and finally, on the third try, grabbed hold of Mistle's sledge and held on tight. Even from a distance I could see his broad shoulders straining with the effort to keep hold of both vehicles.

Sergeant Mistle thrashed her reins again, and the llama attempted to escape, running at full tilt, but Nick hung on, holding the little sledge in place in midair, not letting it get away. Mum was looking over anxiously, trying to control the reindeer with the reins and make sure they didn't pull the sleigh too far to the side, in case Nick was forced to let go.

Still Sergeant Mistle kept trying to pull away, and Nick kept holding her sledge back – the reindeer and the llama all flying their hardest – and everyone was suspended, hundreds of feet in the air. With Mum grasping the reindeer reins with both hands, none of the adults could do anything other than stay exactly where they were.

And as strong as Nick was, there was no way he could hold on to both sleighs forever.

'Will!' I yelled. 'We have to get over there!'

'Come on!' he agreed, patting Starlet on the neck. 'We've got to save our family!'

And we charged through the sky like meteors.

Twenty-two

Nick's grip on the llama-pulled sledge had slowed it down enough for our reindeer to catch up. Amor, with me on her back, raced along the far side of Sergeant Mistle, away from Nick's sleigh, giving a growl that was quite un-reindeer-like, but totally justified.

Sergeant Mistle jumped and squeaked in horror. The snow goggles she wore over her face made her look like an oversized bug. I was relieved to see Yula was firmly strapped into a car seat beside her, and bundled up so warmly against the cold that only the tip of her pink nose was visible. If she wasn't being kidnapped, it would have looked sweet.

Yula spotted me through her fluff and fur and started to reach for me.

'Let her go!' I bellowed at Sergeant Mistle, who was once again trying in vain to drive her flying llama away from Nick and Mum's sleigh.

'I have to take her! It's for the greater good!' Mistle yelled back.

'You're kidnapping her!'

'I'm saving Christmas!' Mistle thrashed her reins and the llama gave a groan of pure annoyance. It craned its neck to look behind at her, with its lip curled back from its prominent teeth.

But Sergeant Mistle didn't seem to have noticed. She was looking from one side of her sledge to the other, as Will, riding Starlet, appeared beside me. Nick was still hanging on to the sledge on the opposite side, sweat breaking out on his brow with the effort. Sergeant Mistle was surrounded.

'You'll never stop me!' she shrieked and wrapped the reins around her hands. She raised them, and with a CRACK that sounded through the night air, whipped the leather straps down on to the llama's back.

That was the final straw for the bewildered llama. Tired, cross and sick of being bashed by the horrible sledge-driver behind it, the llama abruptly stopped. Just *stopped*. It dug its hooves into the night sky like it was the ground and halted so suddenly that we all shot past it: Nick was forced to let go of the little sledge or else have his arm pulled off.

Our reindeer teams paused too, turning in the air to look back at Sergeant Mistle. Her sledge sat there in mid-air, as if it was parked on a road, perfectly still. The llama was staring straight ahead, completely ignoring Sergeant Mistle's shouting and pushing and petulant raging.

The four of us flew back over to the sledge, and quickly

surrounded it once more. Sergeant Mistle huffed out a huge breath and looked as if all the fight had gone out of her. Her shoulders sagged and she looked utterly miserable. Meanwhile, Yula was babbling happily to herself and reached out for Nick as soon as she saw him.

Leaning over, he carefully unbuckled the straps holding the car seat to the little sledge, lifted it out and re-strapped it beside him on the enormous sleigh. Mum immediately started fussing over Yula, who seemed none the worse for her kidnapping.

Sergeant Mistle seemed to shrink as Nick stood up in his sleigh. With one giant stride, he stepped from his vehicle into hers. Mistle shrank back into the seat corner. 'Sir, I—'

'Enough!' Nick said, with a force surer than gravity. 'That's more than enough from you, Sergeant. You think this is part of your *job*? To kidnap children? To steal them away from their family?'

'The magic of Christmas—'

'If the magic of Christmas is disrupted at all this year,' Nick thundered from his great height, 'it will be because of *you*. Your actions, not ours. You, Sergeant Mistle, have forgotten the true meaning of Christmas.'

She went white as a sheet. 'What? No, I never could! I love Christmas! It's my life!'

'Then you had better work out a better way to show it, Tosie Mistle,' Nick said menacingly. He folded his arms. 'Because the golden rule of the Elf and Safety Department is that the true meaning of Christmas must be upheld *above all else*. That's three strikes in one go.'

'What?' she gasped.

'A friendly face on stage reminded me of that, tonight,' Nick said, giving Will and me a nod. 'Tosie Mistle,' he leaned forward, 'I am very, *very* disappointed in you.'

This, more than anything else, seemed to finally get through to the elf. She put her hands over her face, utterly ashamed.

Nick clambered back into his own sleigh and kissed Yula on her forehead, who was still babbling away as if this was just a fun day out. I nudged Amor with my knees and flew closer.

'What time is it?' I asked, suddenly worried. 'It's Christmas Eve . . . hasn't this ruined all your preparations?'

'I honestly don't know if we're going to make it in time for the official take-off,' Nick said seriously, clicking his tongue. 'We're going to need to step on it to get back to the shed. We still need to harness the other reindeer, load the sleigh . . .' He shook his head. He held his hands out, and gently helped me off Amor's back into the sleigh. My legs started aching as soon as I was clear. Nick did the same for Will, and Mum handed us blankets.

'What about the new super-speed on the sleigh?' Will asked, his teeth chattering. 'Won't that help?'

'Ha,' Nick laughed, his expression softening. 'HQ started working on that after they heard about the llama's stand-in role the other year . . . they wanted to make sure we had enough reindeer-power, even if we were an animal down. It'll help get us back to the farm park quickly, but as for loading up and getting ready . . .' He shook his head. 'I'm not even dressed.'

We all looked at each other. Whatever it took, we had to make this happen. Christmas depended on it, Father Christmas depended on *us*! I tried not to imagine what would happen if we failed . . .

There was a soft *whoosh* from beside the sleigh. Tosie Mistle had turned her sledge around, and her red-rimmed eyes were looking straight ahead. 'If I might, sir,' she said quietly. 'I know it's not my place any more, but . . . I think I might have an idea.'

Twenty-three

Before this Christmas, I'd expected elves to be small and cute, wearing little pointy hats with bobbles on the ends. It turns out, nothing is ever how you expect it to be.

'No slacking on the job, Private!' an elf taller than Mum, in a slick black and gold uniform, barked at another who was hurrying past with arms full of wrapped presents. The elf in charge had tattoos on her knuckles that said *GIFT WRAP*. 'The clock is ticking!'

'Yes, madam!' The hurrying elf ran after their colleagues who were loading the sleigh's cargo hold with presents so efficiently and tightly you would have struggled to slide a piece of paper between any of the parcels.

These elves were from T.I.N.S.E.L. – The International NorthPole Sorting Envelopes Logistics division – and they were the most organised people on Planet Earth. Ordinarily, they spent winter sorting the Santa-based letter deliveries, but for the rest of the year they worked in postal systems across the world, making sure we all got our parcels and letters and deliveries.

It turned out that our postie was one of them – she'd been in on our secret all along, even reminded Nick about the true meaning of Christmas when she was on stage. Right now, she was helping two other elves carry something huge over to the back of the sleigh. And although they were all elves, they looked just like ordinary people – the same height, the same variety, and not a pointy ear in sight.

'The idea that all elves look the same is just a rumour

started by the Elf and Safety Department,' Nick explained. He was fitting long-haul flight harnesses on to the reindeer, who were snorting and tossing their heads and eager to be in the sky as soon as possible. 'They come up with fake descriptions to throw people off the right track, you see? No one will think their postie is an elf if he doesn't have pointy ears and boots with curly toes.'

'Sir!' The black-and-gold bedecked elf came over and gave a salute. 'Sir, the cargo hold will reach capacity in the next fifteen minutes, and then we shall ensure the delivery sack is prepped for the first stop of the evening. May I suggest that sir gets his uniform on?'

Nick looked down at his jeans and padded coat. 'Oh, good thinking, Captain.' He quickly finished buckling the harnesses as another elf came up carrying an enormous pile of neatly folded reindeer-skin clothes.

'We've drawn up a makeshift dressing room in the back,' they said. 'Sergeant – I mean, Ms Tosie Mistle, made sure that all your uniform was pressed and ready to go, sir.'

'I can't believe she got all of you to come and help so quickly,' I said.

'Tosie truly believes in the magic of Christmas,' the Captain said. 'Perhaps more than anyone else. And although she often makes rash decisions, she would do anything to preserve it.'

'Including kidnapping a baby?' I pointed out.

The Captain held her hands up. 'We don't agree with what she did. But I believe she is trying to atone for it.' She nodded her head over to the sleigh where Tosie Mistle was ticking endless presents off a list stuck to her clipboard, pointing elves in the right direction, and snapping at anyone and everyone to move as quickly as they could. 'She's learning that not everything can be solved by charts and organisation, even if that is a skill she's very good at putting to use.'

'Christmas isn't about having everything perfectly organised though,' I said. 'It's about your family.' I looked up at Nick. 'Isn't it?'

He nodded. 'I've always thought so.' He gave my shoulder a squeeze. 'Now, I'd better get ready before it gets to midnight . . .' and he hurried away, the elf with his clothes leading the way.

The T.I.N.S.E.L. Captain gave me a smile. 'You know,' she said, 'we've never seen a Claus so happy outside of the Christmas season before.'

'What do you mean?' I asked.

'Well, their purpose is to deliver the presents, spread Christmas cheer and magic, and that only happens for a very short time each year. Outside of that, being Father Christmas can be a rather lonely life. But your family have welcomed Nick in, made a space for him to spread joy and cheer even outside the season. You're right, Harper Hall – Christmas *is* all about your family, whether it's one you've always had, or one you've found. I am very glad that Father Christmas found your family.' She smiled again and gave a small salute, before going to oversee the last few stacks of gifts being loaded into the sleigh.

My chest twinged with feelings, a whole bunch of them all tangled up and filling me to bursting. We were Nick's family, and we always would be. Christmas was a special time of year, but every day was happy when he was around, and when we were all together.

I *did* want him to be there always.

I did want him to be my dad.

*

The sleigh was loaded, the reindeer were harnessed and Nick was dressed in what felt like record time (though I didn't actually have anything to compare it to). The elves of T.I.N.S.E.L. had vanished, ready to carry on their sorting duties in their own offices, and finally it felt like *Christmas*.

Nick looked transformed – somehow even taller and broader than usual, his beard neatly brushed and his long hair loose but tucked down the back of his reindeer-skin coat like a built-in scarf. 'Fancy another ride?' he asked as he heaved himself into the seat of the sleigh.

'I do!' I cried, rushing to clamber up. Will followed after me, and then we both turned and looked at Yula.

To our surprise, she was fast asleep in Mum's arms.

'Huh,' I said. 'Even a Santa Baby gets tired on Christmas Eve.'

'Maybe she can come next year,' Will said, smiling. We settled beside Nick, who gave us a wink.

'Ready? Hold on tight . . .' He tugged on the reins – those strong, rough reins designed to haul a ginormous fully-loaded sleigh – and the reindeer began to run. They charged down the field and dug their hooves into the air, flying upwards into the sky, pulling the sleigh behind them like it weighed nothing.

Will and me waved as hard as we could to Mum, until the ground below looked like a carpet of multicoloured green and brown squares, and we were off to make the most magical deliveries of the year.

Twenty-four

The night air was icy, and the sleigh left vapour trails of snow from its metal skis as it sailed through the sky. The snow fell silently in our wake, drifting down to the ground in snowflakes like tiny pieces of magic, or promises of Christmas.

Nick didn't snap the reins at the reindeer the way Mistle had her llama. He urged them on with his voice, roaring instructions in a language I didn't understand. He only pulled on the reins to steer, or to encourage the reindeer to slow down.

We reached the first set of rooftops quickly, the moonlight giving tiles a pale glow. It was a tiny village, and I could see the cold ripple of the ocean close by.

'This wasn't our first stop last time,' I pointed out.

'I like to keep things fresh every year,' Nick said, clambering out of the sleigh. 'This is Covensea, in the Highlands of Scotland. Stay in the sleigh, won't you?'

We promised, watching as Nick threw back the reindeer-hide tarpaulin that covered the sleigh's cargo hold and lifted out an enormous sack, so big it was a wonder it fit on the sleigh at all.

Nick stepped off the edge of the roof and vanished.

Will turned to me. 'Harper, you called him *Dad*,' he said, only slightly teasingly. 'Back when we were rescuing Yula. I heard you.'

'Shut up,' I muttered, trying to hide in my scarf.

'You did, though.'

'I know.'

'So?' He nudged me, smiling. 'What're you thinking, Harps?'

'I think . . . It's not like a switch I can flick on and off,' I said. 'It's not like I'm certain that *OK, he's my dad now*. I don't know if I can just call him that from now on or not. But . . . I guess . . . he really is my dad. Our dad. In my heart.'

'That's what I've been trying to help you see,' Will said kindly. 'It's not a label, it's something you feel.'

I looked out at the wintry ocean, rippling black and blue in the frozen night. 'Feelings can change in the future.'

'True, but I don't like worrying about what *might* happen,' Will shrugged. 'I like thinking about what *is* happening. And right now, I've got a mum and two sisters and a stepdad . . . dad . . . who are all great. Yes, even you,' he grinned at me. 'It's easy to spend so much time worrying about losing something that you forget to enjoy it whilst it's happening.'

Will was right. Maybe Nick would be around forever. Maybe he wouldn't. But we would always have ridden on Father Christmas's sleigh, always have Yula, always have had the happiest Christmases of our lives. And if Nick felt like a parent . . . then he was one.

'Right then.' Nick was suddenly back on the roof, making us both jump. 'Onwards. Southwards, this time.' He climbed aboard and once again the reindeer hauled themselves skyward, leaving a trail of ice and snow in their wake.

The world was a sleeping toy display, all the houses and cars tiny enough to fit on the head of a pin. The streetlights glowed, casting yellow and orange beams down on to the frosted pavements, and the flashing kaleidoscopes of fairy lights created rainbows in the darkness as we whooshed past, faster than the wind.

Each stop we came to, Nick got out and unloaded the sleigh, carrying presents and toys in an enormous sack that never seemed to get any smaller. The sleigh never ran out of cargo, and there was never a moment we felt lighter as the reindeer pulled their load up into the clouds. Magic filled the air, unseen, essential. Claus magic. The magic our baby sister had.

'What's going to happen to Yula next Christmas?' I asked as we flew over a large body of water that I thought might be the North Sea.

'Babies grow up fast, Harper – I hope enough has happened this year to make Yula more aware of using her powers,' Nick said. 'In a year's time, she should have it under control, more or less. She'll be fine.'

'You sound very confident,' Will called, over the sound of the rushing wind.

'I always am,' Nick replied. 'Everything is alright in the end. And if it's not alright yet, it's not the end.'

A handful more deliveries, and it got too cold for Will and me to stand it much longer. Nick turned the reindeer around and we headed for home, the familiar fields and hedges coming into sight as we descended. I had expected Nick to head for the farm park, but to my surprise he landed us right outside our house. The reindeer clattered on to the road, taking up most of the street, as the sleigh skidded to a halt behind them.

'Someone might see!' I whispered.

'Unlikely,' Nick said with a wink. 'I'm about to do my deliveries. No one will notice a thing. You both get inside and get warm. I'll see you tomorrow.'

'Thank you,' Will said. And after a moment's hesitation, threw his arms around Nick. Nick hugged him back and ruffled his hair.

'Sleep well, William.'

Will jumped down from the sleigh. 'Come on, Harps.'

I looked at Nick. 'Um . . . what I said before . . . when we were trying to get Yula back . . .'

He held a hand up. 'You're allowed to change your

mind, Harper. It's up to you how you see me, what you want to call me. And you don't have to choose something one day and stick to it forever.'

'I know, but . . . sometimes it scares me.' I bit my lip. 'It's always been the three of us. And these past few years, so much has changed. It feels like . . . it could change back. If we're not careful.'

Nick put a hand on my shoulder. 'I'm not going anywhere, Harper Hall. I've spent a long, long time trying to figure out what to do with the other three hundred and sixty-four days of the year. And I've found it.' He glanced behind me at our house. 'I am very, very lucky to have found all of you.'

I smiled. 'You're not going to get sick of us?'

'Not for a second. In fact, I want to ask your . . .' He stopped, and looked nervous for a second.

I suddenly remembered Nick trying to hide something – something very small – the day Yula made the gingerbread people come to life. What if . . . what if it had been . . .

My eyes went wide with excitement. 'Are you going to ask Mum—'

He put a finger to his lips. 'You'll find out tomorrow. Now, go inside! And Merry Christmas.'

My heart beating fast with possibility, I followed Will inside, and closed the door on the silent, still magic of Christmas Eve.

Twenty-five

On Christmas Morning, Yula was much more interested in the boxes and wrapping paper than she was in any of her presents. She kept playing peek-a-boo with the crumpled sheets of paper – laughing her head off, convinced she was invisible when she held the paper up.

'Babies are so weird,' Will said with a smile as he pretended to be shocked that Yula had 'reappeared' again. He handed her a present he had wrapped, and she yanked the paper off in one go, pulling out the hand-knitted jumper with the too-long arms and the lumpy too-small body.

'Very nice, William,' Mum said, kindly.

Yula held it up in one hand, and I thought she might toss it away in boredom, but as we watched, the arms of the jumper began to shrink down and the body grew fatter, until . . .

'Hey, this might actually fit you now!' Will laughed, getting down on the floor to help her put it on. 'Excellent work, Yula.'

Nick arrived just before midday, laden down with last-minute food and gifts and looking tired but extremely happy as he walked into the living room. 'Well, isn't this a wonderful sight,' he said, looking around at the mess of wrapping papers and discarded packaging.

'Merry Christmas!' I cried from one of the heaps.

'MERRRRY CHRISTMAAASS!' he boomed back, his voice a full Santa roar of delight, making all of us burst out laughing.

Dinner was delicious as always, with a mixture of Mum's

experimental cooking and Nick's expert eye combining to make a memorable feast. Yula decided to wear most of her dinner instead of eating it, but nobody minded, and when she waved her hands and turned all the roast potatoes into Christmas-tree-shapes, it was a relief to know that there were no penalties for Christmas magic any more.

I looked around the table, at my brother, my sister and . . . my parents. It was funny, we'd never been incomplete before – we hadn't *needed* Nick and Yula to join us. But it was amazing that they had. We weren't waiting to be made complete, we always had been. We'd just made our group bigger, and with even more love.

*

After dinner, we settled into the living room amongst the opened gifts, the sweets and the soft glow of the television which was showing an old *Doctor Who* Christmas special. One of the characters was having a swordfight in his pyjamas.

'Funny how it all worked out,' Will said, scrunching some paper into a ball. 'And not a single present missed. Those elves were amazing – do you think they could be convinced to do my homework for me?'

Nick and Mum laughed. 'It really was a miracle, getting everything loaded in time,' Mum said. 'I suppose Sergeant Mistle must really value the magic of Christmas. Despite what she did, I do hope she'll be alright.'

'She will be,' Nick said. 'I've asked the T.I.N.S.E.L. Captain to put her in charge of the handwritten letter department. She'll organise them to within an inch of their lives, I have no doubt.'

'I hope she's learnt her lesson,' I said. 'No presents for her for a good long while. She's straight on to the Naughty List.'

'We don't really use that list these days,' Nick said, examining a satsuma. 'Far too much paperwork. I believe it was sometime in 1932 that . . .' He stopped and looked at our faces. 'Too much information?'

'It's hard to believe that Christmas elves are interested in filing and paperwork,' Will teased. 'Think of all the extra present-wrapping time they could get if they didn't do any of that.'

'But then you might miss someone out,' Mum said. 'Or you'd find a present that wasn't for you, under the tree.' She glanced at ours. 'Good job we've cleared ours out completely.'

Nick suddenly went a bit red in the face and cleared his throat. 'There is an extra present, actually.' He got off the sofa, and on to his hands and knees, reaching under the Christmas tree to search.

'Is it for me?' Will asked.

'No,' Nick said, drawing something out. 'No, it's for your mum.'

. . . *Oh! It was really happening!*

I reached out and lifted Yula up off Mum's knee. 'Will, why don't you come and help me in the dining room?' I asked loudly.

Will opened his mouth to ask why, but then saw my expression. 'Um, OK. Sure.'

We quickly walked out, leaving the door open so we could stand by the doorframe and watch and listen to what was about to happen. Even Yula was quiet, her little rosebud mouth open slightly as we peeped around.

For an instant, the scene in the living room was frozen – Nick knelt on one knee, Mum just realising what was happening and Nick's hands clasped together in front of him, hiding something tiny and special.

Will put a hand on my arm.

We couldn't quite hear what was said, but we saw Mum's eyes go huge and round and her mouth drop open. She said something quiet, and then gasped as Nick opened his hands and something sparkled inside a white box.

'He did it,' Will whispered. 'I *knew* he would.'

'What will she say?' I whispered back.

Mum said something, and the two of them burst out laughing, and then Mum was on the floor as well, putting her arms around Nick's shoulders, and they were kissing . . .

'Gross. But I think she said yes,' Will said. 'Or else he's really good at hiding his disappointment.'

'Let's go find out,' I said with a grin, and we leaned our top halves around the doorway like a comedy act.

Nick and Mum spotted us and laughed all over again. 'Did you two know about this?' Mum asked, her eyes shining with happy tears.

'No,' I said honestly. 'But we think it's great!'

'Well, that's good, because it affects all of us,' Mum said, beaming. She held her left hand out, where a ring was now on her finger. It was made of silvery metal, and the stone in the centre was strange – it seemed to flicker as we looked at it, as if it was alive.

I leaned closer to see. Squinting, I could just make it out. It wasn't a diamond or an opal or anything like that – it was a polished dome of crystal, in which a tiny miniature blizzard was flurrying. It wasn't a snow globe – it took no shaking – but a tiny snowstorm, dancing forever on Mum's finger.

'You're going to be Mrs Claus,' Will teased.

Mum scoffed. 'Oh, please. I didn't spend years doing that PhD to be called *Mrs*, thank you very much. It's Dr Hall forever.'

'As it should be.' Nick kissed her on the head.

Yula made a noise then until Nick kissed her as well, and then everyone laughed. I wanted to capture the moment in a snow globe of its own, all five of us together on Christmas Day. But then I realised . . . this was going to be forever. All of our Christmases would be like this, from now on.

Perfectly magical.

Read how it all began in

STEP
FATHER
CHRISTMAS

One

'There's tinsel in my sandwich.'

Mum looked up from the heap of boxes she was in the middle of. 'Well, that's festive.'

I picked the tinsel out from the peanut butter, wondering if it had any nutritional value. I glanced around the room. There was tinsel *everywhere*, along with miniature reindeer, angels and stars, which were scattered over the living room like snow. We were in the middle of putting the Christmas tree up.

Mum extracted herself from the boxes, one hand on

the sideboard to steady herself, trying not to knock over the photo that took pride of place – me, Mum and my big brother Will on Mum's graduation day a few years ago, when she became Dr Helen Hall: Super-Vet. 'I always forget how much Christmas stuff we have until I get it all down from the loft,' she said once she was finally free.

'I think it multiplies up there,' I said. 'I don't remember half of this.'

'I know! Who made this?' She held up an MDF-and-PVA-glue Nativity scene where Mary and Joseph both looked like Shrek. 'Was it Will?'

'No way,' Will answered for me, slouching into the living room, his PuzzoCube glued into his hand as usual. 'I don't draw people like that.' He sat down and began solving the cube without looking up.

'Well, it wasn't me,' I said.

Mum shrugged. 'Maybe it was one of your cousins . . .' She began searching through another bag.

Will pulled a face at me that said *Every year, right?* And I nodded back at him.

Every year, Mum goes as full-on for Christmas as her budget will allow. That's not particularly far, but she always manages to transform the living room into a grotto, complete with hundreds of fairy lights, a massive Christmas tree and so many pillows and rugs you struggle to know where to sit down. When we were little, it was like magic. Now I'm ten, and Will's thirteen, it feels like we've both outgrown it a little — but even though the magic has faded, I haven't said anything to Mum because she loves it so much, and it's always a special family time for the three of us. Mum started going all-out on Christmas back when it was just her and Will, and when I came along it was only a few months before she was dressing me as a baby reindeer for the family photos.

Will twisted his PuzzoCube in his hands.

'Are you winning?' I asked. I was longing to get back

to my own hobby: reading through the latest *Murder at the Tea-Party* storybook I'd got from the library. The main characters are these schoolgirls who run a secret detective agency, and the stories always have these amazing plot twists.

'I'm sort of winning,' Will said, clicking something into place. 'I'm third in the Collectors' League.'

I had no idea what that meant. Will's cube was from the 1970s, a sort of less-successful version of the more famous puzzle cube, where the goal wasn't to get all the colours on the same side, but to copy patterns on collectable cards. He'd picked it up at a jumble sale a few months ago and it had quickly become his obsession.

'Cool,' I said.

'Oh, actually . . .' Mum's head popped up like a jack-in-the-box. 'I'm glad you're in the same room, you two. I wanted to tell you something.' And she suddenly went bright red, like the painted noses on the plastic reindeer.

'What's up?' Will lowered his cube. 'Is it bad?'

'No, no, it's nothing bad,' Mum said, going impossibly redder. 'It's a nice thing.'

'Tell us,' I said. 'Come on, or we'll start guessing.'

Will started guessing anyway. 'Are we being sent to boarding school? Are we getting a dog?'

'No! Sorry, no.' Mum sighed, and brushed some of the dust off her jumper. 'Well . . . Harper, Will . . . we're going to have a guest. For the Christmas season.'

'But we always have Christmas with just the three of us,' I cried.

Will narrowed his eyes. 'Who? What guest?'

'His name's Nick,' Mum said. 'We actually met at Farmer Llama's petting zoo last year, and stayed in touch. He's nice.' She was still as red as a tomato.

'But who *is* he?' I asked. 'Is he working with you?' 'No, he's . . .' Mum twisted an old stocking, then sighed in resignation. 'He's my boyfriend. OK, happy now?'

Me and Will groaned in perfect unison.

Mum doesn't have many boyfriends – she doesn't have time, for starters. Because she's a vet, she's always zooming out the house to go and see to people's sick dogs or cats or stick insects. The last boyfriend who Will and I met, Disaster Dave, used to build cathedrals out of spent matches, and even now we still find empty matchboxes stuffed into the backs of drawers and used as bookmarks. But we hadn't met one of her boyfriends for a long time. Years, actually. The thought of Mum seeing someone seriously was . . . *weird*.

'What's he like?' I asked, as Will went back to his puzzle.

Mum beamed in response. 'Oh, he's ever so nice. A real gent. He loves animals, and works seasonally up at Farmer Llama's.'

'Oh.' As stories went, it wasn't exactly thrilling.

'When's he coming?'

'He'll be round this afternoon for a cup of tea' – Mum checked her watch – 'and to meet you and Will, of course. And as long as we all get on, he'll be staying here for a few weeks.'

I wasn't sure I liked the idea of there being a stranger in the house, but if Mum liked him enough to keep in touch for a whole year, he must be nice. I nodded. 'OK then.'

Mum's smile softened a bit. 'Thanks for being understanding, Harper. He won't be under your feet. He leaves very early and often comes home very late, because of the animals. But you're being really kind – I know it's not cool to think about your mum having a boyfriend.'

Will muttered something under his breath, but Mum either didn't hear or pretended not to.

We carried on wrestling with putting the tree up, Will peeling himself away from his PuzzoCube long enough to put the star on top as he was the tallest. We'd just tidied some of the boxes away and were in the kitchen putting the kettle on when the doorbell rang.

Mum went white, then red, then white again like a malfunctioning candy cane. 'Oh, he's early!'

'Tell him to wait,' Will said, stuffing bags-for-life into the cupboard under the stairs.

'I can't do that, Will, don't be silly. Just clear some space on the sofa for him to sit. Harper, will you sort out the teapot?' She bustled off to the door, tinsel trailing from where it was stuck to one of her sleeves.

Will looked at me, shaking his head. 'She must really like him.'

'I hope he's normal,' I said, pouring the boiling water. 'Not another one with a weird hobby.'

The front door opened, and I heard laughter and a man's voice. Will scuttled away into the living room and I put the lid on the teapot just as Mum came into the kitchen.

'. . . and this is Harper,' she said, happily.

I put on my brightest smile and turned to say hello.

Except the word never made it out of my mouth.

'Hello there, Harper,' Nick said in a quiet but friendly way. But although my mouth was open, I still couldn't speak because I was too stunned.

The man in front of me . . . my mum's new boyfriend . . . he had grey-white hair, a white beard, a comfy round stomach and was wearing red trousers and big black boots . . .

'Merry Christmas,' he said with a smile.

Read on in *Stepfather Christmas* – OUT NOW!

Acknowledgements

A Very Merry Christmas and a huge bundle of thanks for the help in bringing this book to life firstly goes to not one but *two* editors – Lena McCauley and Lizzie Clifford. Thank you for giving Harper and the gang another adventure.

Shoutout to all the amazing booksellers who helped and supported *Stepfather Christmas*, including but not limited to: Helen, Dion, Robbie, Jamie-Lee, Ruth, Lydia, Nick and Mel, and everyone at Waterstones Nottingham. You helped Nick's sleigh to fly.

Thanks as always to my amazing publicity and marketing teams, particularly to Dom, Beth and Katie for always being ding-dong-merrily on high, and organising me better than any bunch of elves. And all the ribbons and bows of celebration must go to designer Sam and illustrator Rachael for the wonderful cover that brings all the festive cheer and delight!

To Claire Wilson, I owe you my life once more, but I hope you'll settle for a few new stories! Thank you for always being there for me, for my characters, and for the complete nonsense I roll into your inbox every so often.

And to Anton and Joseph . . . it's been a year of huge changes and big moves, and I am so glad we are a team together. Thank you for everything. Merry Christmas, my boys.

About the Author

L. D. Lapinski lives just outside Sherwood Forest with
their family, a lot of books, and a cat called Hector.
They are the author of *The Strangeworlds Travel Agency* series,
Stepfather Christmas, *Artezans: The Forgotten Magic* first
in a new series, and the standalone *Jamie*.

When they aren't writing, L. D. can be found cosplaying,
drinking a lot of cherry cola, and taking care of a forest of
succulent plants. L. D. first wrote a book aged seven; it was
made of lined paper and Sellotape, and it was about a frog
who owned an aeroplane. When L. D. grows up, they want
to be a free-range guinea pig farmer.

You can find them on social media @ldlapinski or at ldlapinski.com

AT THE

STRANGEWORLDS

· TRAVEL AGENCY ·

EACH SUITCASE TRANSPORTS YOU TO
A DIFFERENT WORLD. ALL YOU HAVE
TO DO IS STEP INSIDE . . .

'FABULOUS, HOPEFUL, IMPORTANT'
Emma Carroll

JAMIE

L. D. LAPINSKI

A joyful story of bravery, acceptance and
finding your place in the world.

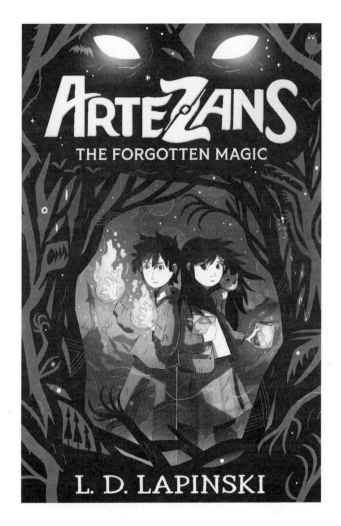

ARTEZZANS
THE FORGOTTEN MAGIC

L. D. LAPINSKI

For the last 400 years magic has been fading . . .
but two extraordinary twins are bringing it back!
Get ready for the magical adventure of your dreams.

OUT NOW